C000171053

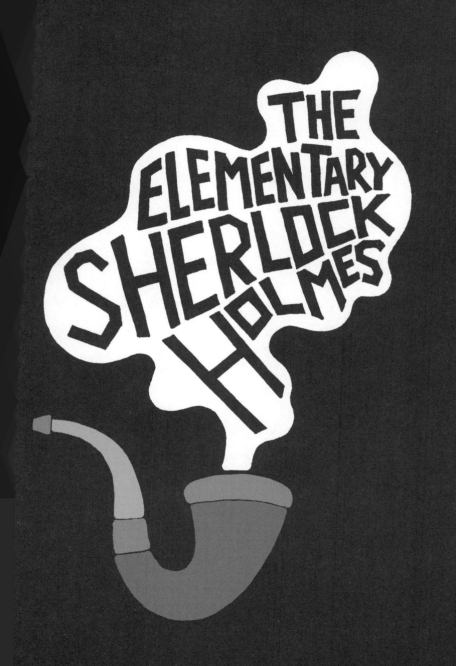

# THE ELEMENTARY SHERLOCK HOLMES

THINGS YOU DIDN'T KNOW ABOUT LITERATURE'S GREATEST DETECTIVE

PORTICO

First published in the United Kingdom in 2014 by
Portico
1 Gower Street
London
WC1E 6HD

An imprint of Pavilion Books Company Ltd

ISBN 978-1-90939-699-9

A CIP catalogue record for this book is available from
the British Library.

10 9 8 7 6 5 4 3 2 1

Reproduction by Mission Productions Ltd, Hong Kong
Printed and bound by GPS Group Ltd, Slovenia

This book can be ordered direct from the publisher at
www.pavilionbooks.com

Based on *The Sherlock Holmes Encyclopedia*.

# CONTENTS

As Holmes himself said, 'Education never ends,' so if your knowledge of Sherlock is less than comprehensive, I deduce that *The Elementary Sherlock Holmes* is precisely what you need.

# INTRODUCTION

If you've watched Benedict Cumberbatch in the excellent BBC series *Sherlock* and found yourself wondering: 'Yes, but how many Baker Street Irregulars *were* there?' then this is the book for you. Or if you occasionally ask yourself, 'I wonder how many times a butler appears in the stories?' then this is the book for you. Or if you'd like to know what Sherlock *really* thought of women, then this is the book for you.

Perhaps you know that your brother-in-law's knowledge of the Great Detective needs brushing up with a potted version of all Conan Doyle's 56 short stories and 4 novels (and a cheat's guide to whodunnit in all of them at the end) – if so, this is the book for him. And if your neighbour confessed to you the other day that she didn't know the significance of Arthur Conan Doyle's father's middle name, then this is definitely the book for her.

And for anyone who wants to find out more about the Victorian world of Sherlock Holmes, Dr Watson, Mycroft, Moriarty, Mrs Hudson and Inspector Lestrade, and the continuing legacy of Doyle's most famous creation in the areas of literature, film, TV and radio, this book will enlighten, amuse and entertain.

# SHERLOCK HOLMES

## YOUNG SHERLOCK

Little is known with any high degree of certainty about the early life and family of Sherlock Holmes, the world's first consulting detective. His ancestors were country squires and one of his grandmothers was the sister of the French artist Vernet – 'Art in the blood is liable to take the strangest forms' ('The Greek Interpreter'). He was born in 1853 or 1854 (he was 60 years old in 'His Last Bow', set in August 1914). He attended university for two years, solving his first case while an undergraduate ('The *Gloria Scott*'). A friend's father is so impressed with his powers of deduction that he plants a seed by suggesting Holmes makes a career of it; Sherlock tells Watson that it 'made me feel that a profession might be made out of what had up to that time been the merest hobby'.

Although many authors have speculated since on what might have happened in his formative years, these are the only facts we learn from the stories about Sherlock's life before he leaves university.

## SHERLOCK BEFORE THE FALL(S)

When Watson and Holmes agreed to share lodgings at Baker Street, the Great Detective's career was presumably still in its infancy, hence his need to share the cost with another. By 1889, however, Holmes was able to say (in *The Hound of the Baskervilles*) that he had investigated some 500 cases 'of capital importance', and just two years later he claimed (in 'The Final Problem') to have worked on a thousand cases. By now he was famous throughout Europe and had conducted investigations for several monarchs.

Holmes told his friend in 'The Final Problem', 'Your memoirs will draw to an end, Watson, upon the day that I crown my career by the capture or extinction of the most dangerous and capable criminal in Europe.' The demise of Moriarty gave Sherlock the opportunity to relinquish his role as the Great Detective by allowing Watson, and hence the rest of the world, to believe he had joined the Napoleon of Crime at the bottom of the Reichenbach Falls.

## THE GREAT HIATUS

This is the name given to the three-year period between Sherlock's supposed death in Switzerland and his triumphant return in 'The Empty House'. During this time he tells Watson he has been in Tibet, Mecca, Khartoum and Montpellier under the alias 'Sigerson', until the murder of Ronald Adair drew him back to London. He only told Mycroft he was alive, and that only because he needed money from him.

## LATER CAREER

Between his return in 1894 and his retirement around ten years later, Holmes solved hundreds of cases, including one ('The Bruce-Partington Plans') that earned him a private audience at Windsor with Queen Victoria, from which he returned with a handsome emerald tiepin. In June 1902 he declined a knighthood, and it seems he retired the following year. Certainly in December 1904 Watson announced to readers of *Strand Magazine* (in 'The Second Stain') that Holmes had 'definitely retired from London and betaken himself to study and bee-farming on the Sussex Downs'.

## RETIREMENT

Holmes spent his retirement on a small farm five miles from Eastbourne, dividing his time between 'philosophy and agriculture' – a suitably Sherlockian combination. Despite turning down all employment including some princely offers during his twilight years, such was the crisis facing his country in the years before the start of the First World War that Holmes acquiesced to the request of the prime minister and returned to service. His task – to penetrate the spy ring of the German intelligence master Von Bork ('His Last Bow'). Although Watson continued to chronicle mysteries Sherlock had solved before his retirement, 'His Last Bow' was the Great Detective's final case.

## DEATH

Nowhere in the stories is mention made of the final passing of Sherlock Holmes. There appeared in the December 1948 issue of *Strand* an obituary for Holmes written by E.V. Knox; coming a mere two years before the demise of the magazine itself, the obituary was more a product of postwar pessimism than a legitimate termination of interest in the detective.

His passing, whenever it occurred, could not have been better marked than by Dr Watson, who wrote in 1891 after Reichenbach that Holmes was 'the best and the wisest man' he ever knew.

## SHERLOCK IN HIS OWN WORDS

*I am the last and highest court of appeal in detection.*
THE SIGN OF FOUR

*I am a brain, Watson. The rest of me is a mere appendix.*
'THE MAZARIN STONE'

*I am the most incurably lazy devil that ever stood in shoe leather.*
A STUDY IN SCARLET

*I am not the law, but I represent justice so far as my feeble powers go.*
'THE THREE GABLES'

*It is fortunate for this community that I am not a criminal.*
'THE BRUCE-PARTINGTON PLANS'

## SHERLOCK IN DR WATSON'S WORDS

*The most perfect reasoning and observing machine that the world has seen...*
'A SCANDAL IN BOHEMIA'

*I have not heard him laugh often, and it has always boded ill to somebody.*
THE HOUND OF THE BASKERVILLES

*You really are an automaton — a calculating-machine ... There is something positively inhuman in you at times.*
THE SIGN OF FOUR

*The best and the wisest man whom I have ever known.*
'THE FINAL PROBLEM'

14

# FAMOUS PORTRAYALS OF SHERLOCK HOLMES

The list of well-known actors who have played Holmes is a long one and includes such famous and unlikely names as Buster Keaton, John Barrymore, Raymond Massey, Christopher Lee, Stewart Granger, John Cleese, Leonard Nimoy, Larry Hagman, Roger Moore, Peter Cook, Christopher Plummer, Tom Baker, Ian Richardson, Charlton Heston and Edward Woodward, as well as the following.

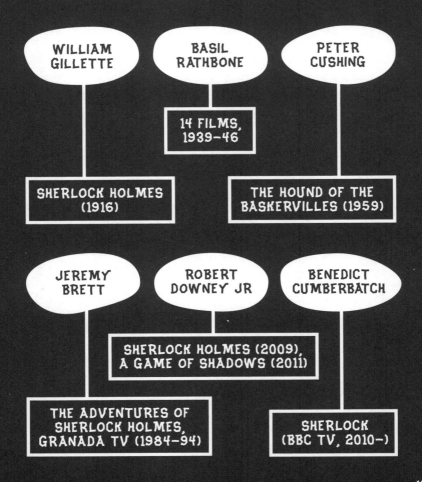

# DOGS

A number of memorable dogs appear in the stories, serving as both weapons of justice and of crime. The most notable canine in all of Watson's writings was the Hound of the Baskervilles, supposedly a hound from hell that cursed the Baskerville family of Dartmoor, but actually was described by Watson as a cross between a wolfhound and a mastiff, coated in phosphorus. Other dogs in the stories included:

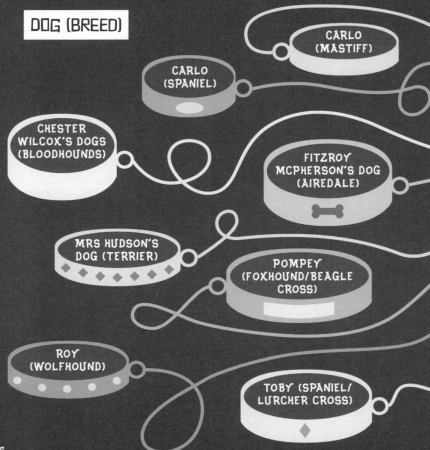

DOG (BREED)

CARLO (MASTIFF)

CARLO (SPANIEL)

CHESTER WILCOX'S DOGS (BLOODHOUNDS)

FITZROY MCPHERSON'S DOG (AIREDALE)

MRS HUDSON'S DOG (TERRIER)

POMPEY (FOXHOUND/BEAGLE CROSS)

ROY (WOLFHOUND)

TOBY (SPANIEL/LURCHER CROSS)

WATSON'S DOG
(BULL-PUP)

# SHERLOCK HOLMES IN FILM

Sherlock Holmes has probably been portrayed on the big screen more than any other fictional character. The cinema juggernaut started to roll with the short silent film *Sherlock Holmes Baffled* dating from around 1900, and by 2014 the Great Detective (as well as some rather odd versions of him/her) had clocked up getting on for 170 appearances, according to the Internet Movie Database. Here are some of the best remembered.

### The Hound of the Baskervilles (1939)

Still perhaps many people's favourite Holmes film of all, this moody, fog-filled feature was Basil Rathbone's debut in the role that defined him. No one predicted the huge impact the character would have – 20th Century Fox gave Richard Greene, playing Sir Henry Baskerville, top billing, and the movie poster featured not Holmes, but the hound!

### The Hound of the Baskervilles (1959)

This well-received Hammer film was the first Holmes film released in colour and starred Peter Cushing. True to form, the horror company weren't afraid to tinker with details to make the story even more juicy than the original, tossing in the odd ritual sacrifice and tarantula to spice things up.

### The Private Life of Sherlock Holmes (1970)

A box-office flop, this is notable mainly for Christopher Lee's appearance as Mycroft Holmes, making him the first (and so far only) person to portray both brothers on screen, having first played Sherlock in a 1962 German film.

### The Adventures of Sherlock Holmes' Smarter Brother (1975)

Douglas Wilmer plays Sherlock but is predictably upstaged by
Gene Wilder as his hitherto-unknown younger brother Sigerson
Holmes in a musical-comedy spoof that failed to hit the same high
notes as Wilder's appearances in *Young Frankenstein* and *Blazing
Saddles*. The name Sigerson is taken from an alias used by Holmes
in 'The Empty House'.

### The Seven-Per-Cent Solution (1976)

Based on the Nicholas Meyer novel of the same name, this was
a stylish attempt to explore the relationship of Holmes (Nicol
Williamson) with cocaine, and introduces the Great Detective to
Sigmund Freud.

### Murder by Decree (1979)

Sherlock Holmes (Christopher Plummer) tackles Jack the Ripper,
Freemasonry and corruption at the heart of government in one of
the finest of all Holmes films.

### Without a Clue (1988)

In this entertaining comedy a bumbling Sherlock (Michael Caine)
is hired by the brilliant Dr Watson (Ben Kingsley) to act as a front
man, allowing the doctor to solve crimes surreptitiously. When
Watson becomes jealous of Holmes's fame and tries to kill him off,
he encounters the same problems as Conan Doyle.

### Sherlock Holmes (2009)

Guy Ritchie's action-packed feature predictably favoured duels and
dust-ups over deduction, but the pairing of Robert Downey Jr and
Jude Law as Holmes and Watson was a big hit at the box office.
The 2011 sequel *Game of Shadows* also played well, and a third
Downey & Law Holmes movie is planned.

# SHERLOCK ICONS

### VIOLIN

Apart from cocaine and tobacco, music was Sherlock's great diversion. He owned a Stradivarius worth at least £500 that he purchased on Tottenham Court Road for 55 shillings, an instrument that helped him outwit Count Sylvius in 'The Mazarin Stone'. He is always picking up his violin, and seems an accomplished player from Watson's accounts.

## DEERSTALKER AND CAPE

The majority of Sherlock fans would immediately identify him by his cap and cape, but in the stories he only wore them for cases that took him to the country. Watson, however, never specifically identified the headgear as a deerstalker, only describing 'his long grey travelling cloak and close-fitting cloth cap' ('The Boscombe Valley Mystery'). It was left to illustrator Sidney Paget to begin the association of Holmes with the deerstalker.

## PIPE

Probably Sherlock's most recognisable possession, described by Watson, sketched in the accompanying illustrations and appearing in film and onstage. Although he is now most associated with the distinctive curved meerschaum pipe, actually he had a litter of pipes scattered over the mantelpiece in his bedroom, and kept others in the coal scuttle. His tobacco was stored in, among other places, the toe end of a Persian slipper. Holmes sometimes measured the difficulty of his cases in terms of his pipe – the puzzle of the Red-Headed League was 'quite a three-pipe problem'.

## FIRST PUBLISHED

* * * * * * * * * * * * * * * * * * *

*Mrs Beeton's Christmas Annual*, 1887; published as a novel 1888

## MAJOR PLAYERS

* * * * * * * * * * * * * * * * * * *

Holmes, Watson, Lestrade, Gregson, Enoch Drebber, Jefferson Hope, Joseph Ferrier, Lucy Ferrier

# MYSTERY

The first Sherlock Holmes story to be published, *A Study in Scarlet* was notable for detailing the first meeting between Holmes and Watson at St Bartholomew's. Divided into two parts, in the first Sherlock investigates the murders first of Enoch Drebber and then Joseph Stangerson. The former is both mysterious and gruesome, providing Holmes with ample opportunity to demonstrate his powers as a detective. In what will become a recurring theme of Sherlock's career, the Scotland Yard detectives arrest the wrong man. Holmes' solution of the crime leads to Part Two, a third-person account of the adventures and tragedy endured by John Ferrier, his adopted daughter Lucy and their friend Jefferson Hope; the Mormon community of Utah serves as a backdrop to the narrative. The final two chapters allow Holmes to explain the solution and wrap up the last details of the case. He calls it 'our study in scarlet', so-called because of 'the scarlet thread of murder running through the colourless skein of life'.

When Watson urges Holmes to publish an account of the tale, adding, 'If you won't, I will,' Sherlock passes him the newspaper report giving all the credit to Lestrade and Gregson. Watson insists: 'I have all the facts in my journal, and the public shall know them.'

# DISGUISES OF SHERLOCK HOLMES

*'The stage lost a fine actor . . .*
*when he became a specialist in crime.'*

('A SCANDAL IN BOHEMIA')

Sherlock Holmes was, famously, a master of disguise, and had at least five safe houses in London where he could change his appearance to suit his circumstances. His new character often fooled Watson himself (no difficult feat if Sherlock's assessment of his companion's powers of observation are any guide), and included the following.

| DISGUISE | STORY |
|---|---|
| Elderly deformed man Watson bumps into | 'The Empty House' |
| Italian priest Watson meets on a train | 'The Final Problem' |
| French *ouvrier* who rescues Watson from an assault | 'The Disappearance of Lady Carfax' |
| Drunken-looking groom | 'A Scandal in Bohemia' |
| Asthmatic old mariner who sits in Holmes's study next to Watson for a while | The Sign of Four |
| Opium smoker who approaches Watson in a drugs den | 'The Man with the Twisted Lip' |

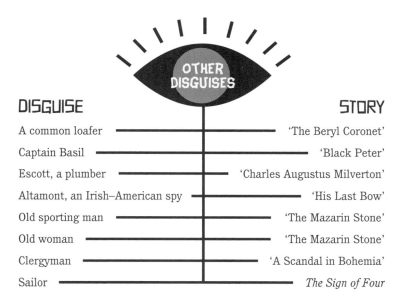

## DISGUISE

A common loafer ———————————— 'The Beryl Coronet'

Captain Basil ———————————— 'Black Peter'

Escott, a plumber ———————————— 'Charles Augustus Milverton'

Altamont, an Irish–American spy ——————— 'His Last Bow'

Old sporting man ———————————— 'The Mazarin Stone'

Old woman ———————————— 'The Mazarin Stone'

Clergyman ———————————— 'A Scandal in Bohemia'

Sailor ———————————— *The Sign of Four*

## STORY

## THE EAGLE-EYED WATSON'S REACTION

'it struck me that the fellow must be some poor bibliophile'

'Good heavens,' I cried; 'How you startled me!'

'I turned to thank my preserver'

'I had to look three times before I was indeed certain it was he'

'Holmes! . . . You here! But where is the old man?'

'It took all my self-control to prevent me from breaking out into a cry of astonishment'

# 221B BAKER STREET

The earliest description of the suite of rooms up the 17 stairs that Watson has failed to count ('A Scandal in Bohemia') at 221B Baker Street is from *A Study in Scarlet*: 'a couple of comfortable bedrooms and a single large airy sitting-room, comfortably furnished'. Mrs Hudson presumably occupied the entire ground floor.

Much to the disappointment of early Sherlock devotees who might have made the pilgrimage, there was no 221 Baker Street, let alone a 221B. In Holmes' time, Baker Street was short, barely over a quarter of a mile, and house numbers only got up to No. 85. In 1930, however, the entire length of the thoroughfare was renamed Baker Street, requiring a renumbering.

A Georgian house, No. 41 Upper Baker Street, was redesignated 221 Baker Street, but was demolished the same year to make room for Abbey House, and Nos. 215–229 became the HQ of the Abbey Road (later the Abbey National) Building Society. They soon had to employ a secretary purely for the purpose of answering the thousands of letters that would arrive each year addressed to Sherlock Holmes.

In 1990 the Sherlock Holmes Museum opened just down the street at No. 239 Baker Street. In a highly unusual step, it was granted permission by the council to be officially numbered 221B.

# ERRORS AND INCONSISTENCIES

Having written 60 Holmes stories over the course of nearly 40 years, it's understandable that Conan Doyle let the odd mistake and contradiction slip through here and there. Here are a few of the most obvious questions thrown up.

In 'The Final Problem' we first meet Professor Moriarty, and also his brother, Colonel James Moriarty. But in 'The Empty House' we learn Professor Moriarty's first name – James. Why would both brothers have the same first name?

In 'The Red-Headed League', Wilson sees the advertisement on 27 April, has worked for the League for eight weeks and Watson confirms it was 'two months ago' – this gives a date of late June for the story. But then Wilson says the notice on the door dissolving the League was dated 9 October, over five months after the date of the advertisement. (As the story opens 'in the autumn', we must assume that it is the April date that is in error.)

Everyone knows that Dr Watson is called John. So why, in 'The Man with the Twisted Lip', does his wife call him James?

In 'The Three Students' Holmes identifies a 'Johann Faber' pencil because of the 'NN' remaining at the stub. But what has happened to the word 'FABER'?

In 'Wisteria Lodge' Watson says the events began in March 1892 – but Holmes supposedly fell into the Reichenbach Falls in 1891, and doesn't re-appear until 1894.

In *A Study in Scarlet*, Watson's war wound was caused by being 'struck on the shoulder by a Jezail bullet'. But in *The Sign of Four* he is 'sat nursing my wounded leg, I had a Jezail bullet through it some time before'.

In 'The Final Problem', set in 1891 just before Moriarty's death, Watson has never heard of him, but in *The Valley of Fear* Moriarty is alive and Watson is already familiar with the name.

In fairness to the author, I dare say Doyle would put most of these mistakes down to a slipshod copy-editor.

## FIRST PUBLISHED

- - - - - - - - - - - - - - - - - -

*Lippincott's Monthly Magazine*, February 1890 (as 'The Sign of the Four'); published as a novel in October 1890

## MAJOR PLAYERS

- - - - - - - - - - - - - - - - - -

Holmes, Watson, Mary Morstan, Thaddeus Sholto, Bartholomew Sholto, Jonathan Small, Inspector Athelney Jones, Tonga, Toby

# MYSTERY

One of the most famous cases investigated by
Holmes, it is actually comprised of two tales. The first
is the complex puzzle of the death of Bartholomew Sholto
and the subsequent theft of the Agra Treasure. The second
is the romance between Watson and Sherlock's client, Mary
Morstan, whose father Arthur disappeared mysteriously ten years
ago. The investigation is one of the finest of Holmes' illustrious
career as he pursues the murderers from the terrible crime scene at
Pondicherry Lodge to the Thames. The climax involves a danger-
filled chase down the river, during which Holmes kills a human
being directly for the first and only time in the chronicles.
The narrative opens and closes with a straight-
forward reference to Sherlock's cocaine habit,
of which Watson clearly disapproves.

# BUTLERS

As Holmes frequently dealt with England's upper classes, it was inevitable that he should encounter a number of butlers. While most of these were unremarkable, several were quite memorable, perhaps none more so than Barrymore, the butler at Baskerville Hall.

| NAME | PLACE OF SERVICE |
| --- | --- |
| Ames | Birlstone Manor House |
| Anthony | Merripit House |
| Bannister | St Luke's College |
| Barrymore, John | Baskerville Hall |
| Brunton, Richard | Hurlstone |
| Hudson | Donnithorpe Estate |
| Jacobs | Whitehall Terrace |
| John | The home of Dr Leslie Armstrong |
| Jose | Manservant of Don Murillo |
| Khitmutgar | The homes of Thaddeus and Bartholomew Sholto |
| Old Ralph | Tuxbury Old Hall |
| Staples | The home of Culverton Smith |
| Stephens | Shoscombe Old Place |

Not counting several unnamed menservants mentioned in various adventures, and a poor anonymous 'native butler' beaten to death in India by the unspeakable Grimesby Roylett, here are the butlers Sherlock encounters.

## CASE

# SHERLOCK AND COCAINE

Holmes was long under the influence of the highly addictive stimulant, from which Dr Watson was apparently successful in freeing him. The earliest indications that Holmes might have been using some kind of drug were given in the very first Holmes story, *A Study in Scarlet*, where it appears Watson is in denial at what he is seeing. Holmes lies around for days on end, and the doctor says, 'I have noticed such a dreamy, vacant expression in his eyes, that I might have suspected him of being addicted to the use of some narcotic, had not the temperament and cleanliness of his whole life forbidden such a notion.'

However, by the opening paragraph of the next book, *The Sign of Four*, Watson has been entirely disabused as he describes Sherlock injecting himself with a hypodermic and adds, 'Three times a day for many months I had witnessed this performance.' There is no doubting Watson's disapproval, as he cautions him that 'the game is hardly worth the candle'. He calls Holmes a 'self-poisoner' ('The Five Orange Pips') and stresses to him the dangers of taking cocaine ('The Man with the Twisted Lip'). After Sherlock's much-delayed return from his duel with Moriarty at Reichenbach, Watson seems satisfied that his gradual weaning of his friend from the drug is working, though he admits that 'the fiend was not dead but sleeping'.

Holmes' addiction naturally received little attention in early films featuring the detective, so it was a shock to hear Basil Rathbone's detective exclaim at the end of *The Hound of the Baskervilles* (1939), 'Oh, Watson, the needle!' By far the most serious examination of the addiction was by Nicholas Meyer in his novel *The Seven-Per-Cent Solution* (1974) and its film version two years later. The BBC's current popular reworking of the stories starring Benedict Cumberbatch and Martin Freeman so far seems to be steering clear of tackling the issue, perhaps for fear of glamorising it.

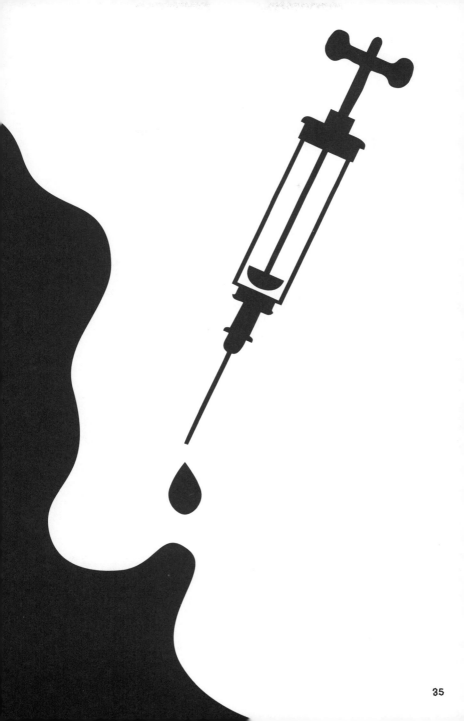

# THE WRITINGS OF SHERLOCK HOLMES

Sherlock enthusiasts should be grateful that so many of
Dr Watson's reminiscences have been preserved, but considering
what a prolific writer Holmes himself was, what a find it would
be if one of the following – perhaps the 10 most riveting –
ever turned up in someone's collection:

UPON THE DISTINCTION
BETWEEN THE ASHES OF
THE VARIOUS TOBACCOS:
AN ENUMERATION OF
THE 140 FORMS OF
CIGAR, CIGARETTE AND
PIPE TOBACCO, WITH
COLOURED PLATES
ILLUSTRATING THE
DIFFERENCES IN THE ASH

THE TRACING
OF FOOTSTEPS,
WITH SOME
REMARKS UPON
THE USES OF
PLASTER OF
PARIS AS A
PRESERVER
OF IMPRESSES

ON
TATTOO
MARKS

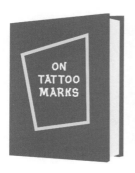

A STUDY OF THE INFLUENCE
OF A TRADE UPON THE
FORM OF THE HAND,
WITH LITHOTYPES OF
THE HANDS OF SLATERS,
SAILORS, CORK-CUTTERS,
COMPOSITORS, WEAVERS
AND DIAMOND-CUTTERS

EXPLORATIONS
IN TIBET
(published under the
name Sigerson, a
Norwegian explorer)

A STUDY
OF THE
CHALDEAN
ROOTS IN
THE ANCIENT
CORNISH
LANGUAGE

TWO SHORT
MONOGRAPHS
ON THE
VARIATIONS
IN THE SHAPE OF
THE HUMAN EAR

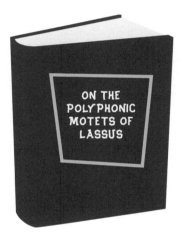

ON THE
POLYPHONIC
MOTETS OF
LASSUS

PRACTICAL
HANDBOOK OF
BEE CULTURE,
WITH SOME
OBSERVATIONS
UPON THE
SEGREGATION
OF THE QUEEN

THE TYPEWRITER AND
ITS RELATION TO CRIME
(probably unpublished)

# MYCROFT HOLMES

Sherlock's elder brother, who possessed greater powers of observation than his sibling but who lacked both energy and ambition. Although one of the most compelling figures in the Holmes stories, he actually appears in only two – 'The Greek Interpreter' and 'The Bruce-Partington Plans' – and is referred to in just two others ('The Final Problem' and 'The Empty House'). Despite his frequent presence in some adaptations (for example Mark Gatiss's enigmatic portrayal in the recent BBC version), his appearance at Baker Street in the original stories was rare: 'as if you met a tram-car coming down a country lane'.

Mycroft was the only person who knew that Holmes was still alive after the terrible events at the Reichenbach Falls in 1891, maintaining the Baker Street lodgings and providing his brother with any money he required. He was seven years older than Sherlock, had an 'absolutely corpulent' body, and spent most of his day at the famously Trappist Diogenes Club. Despite all this, according to Sherlock his brother is a key government adviser, indeed 'occasionally he *is* the British government'.

## SHERLOCK ON MYCROFT

'His specialism is omniscience'

'The most indispensable man in the country'

## MYCROFT ON SHERLOCK

'Sherlock has all the energy of the family'

## WATSON ON MYCROFT

'Above this unwieldy frame there was perched a head so masterful in its brow … that after the first glance one forgot the gross body and remembered only the dominant mind'

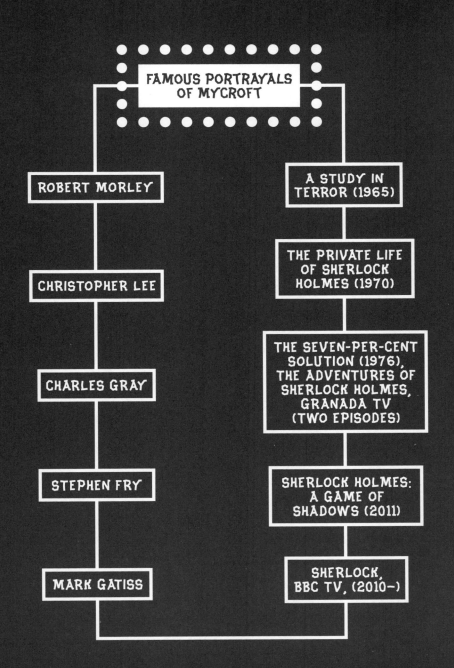

FAMOUS PORTRAYALS
OF MYCROFT

ROBERT MORLEY

CHRISTOPHER LEE

CHARLES GRAY

STEPHEN FRY

MARK GATISS

A STUDY IN
TERROR (1965)

THE PRIVATE LIFE
OF SHERLOCK
HOLMES (1970)

THE SEVEN-PER-CENT
SOLUTION (1976),
THE ADVENTURES OF
SHERLOCK HOLMES,
GRANADA TV
(TWO EPISODES)

SHERLOCK HOLMES:
A GAME OF
SHADOWS (2011)

SHERLOCK,
BBC TV, (2010–)

# SHERLOCK'S BEST QUOTES

As you might expect of a man who didn't suffer fools gladly, Sherlock rarely seemed to speak a word that wasn't weighed carefully for its impact. Consequently he remains eminently quotable.

*It is stupidity rather than courage to refuse to recognize danger when it is close upon you.*

'THE FINAL PROBLEM'

MORIARTY *If you are clever enough to bring destruction upon me, rest assured that I shall do as much to you.*

HOLMES *If I were assured of the former eventuality I would, in the interest of the public, cheerfully accept the latter.*

'THE FINAL PROBLEM'

*Beyond the obvious facts that he has at some time done manual labour, that he takes snuff, that he is a Freemason, that he has been in China, and that he has done a considerable amount of writing lately, I can deduce nothing else.*

'THE RED-HEADED LEAGUE'

INSPECTOR GREGORY *Is there any point to which you wish to draw my attention?*

HOLMES *To the curious incident of the dog in the night-time.*

GREGORY *The dog did nothing in the night-time.*

HOLMES *That was the curious incident.*

'SILVER BLAZE'


*It is my business to know what other people don't know.*

'THE BLUE CARBUNCLE'


*Education never ends, Watson. It is a series of lessons, with the greatest for the last.*

'THE RED CIRCLE'

41

# THE ADVENTURES OF SHERLOCK HOLMES

Published in 1892, this volume was the first collection of the detective's cases that had originally appeared in *Strand Magazine* and was dedicated to Doyle's 'old teacher' Joseph Bell, considered the inspiration or model for Holmes.

## 'A Scandal in Bohemia'

**FIRST PUBLISHED** *Strand Magazine*, July 1891

**MAJOR PLAYERS** Holmes, Watson, the King of Bohemia, Irene Adler

**MYSTERY** Unusual in that Holmes is outwitted, and by a woman! Despite his best efforts on behalf of the king to retrieve an incriminating photograph in Adler's possession, he is thwarted, although all turns out well. He is left with a gold snuffbox from the king and his own photo of 'the woman', the admirable Irene Adler.

## 'The Red-Headed League'

**FIRST PUBLISHED** *Strand Magazine*, August 1891

**MAJOR PLAYERS** Holmes, Watson, Jabez Wilson, John Clay (Vincent Spaulding), Duncan Ross, Peter Jones, Mr Merryweather

**MYSTERY** A flame-haired pawnbroker is paid a generous sum to vacate his premises on a regular basis in order to copy out the encyclopedia at the offices of the Red-Headed League. When the League dissolves without warning, the perplexed pawnbroker turns to Holmes.

## 'A Case of Identity'

**FIRST PUBLISHED** *Strand Magazine*, September 1891

**MAJOR PLAYERS** Holmes, Watson, Mary Sutherland, Hosmer Angel, Mr Windibank

**MYSTERY** Holmes is hired by Mary Sutherland to find her elusive fiancé Hosmer Angel, who has vanished from the cab carrying him to their wedding. Holmes learns that Mary knew very little of her intended, not even where he lived…

## 'The Boscombe Valley Mystery'

**FIRST PUBLISHED** *Strand Magazine*, October 1891

**MAJOR PLAYERS** Holmes, Watson, Lestrade, James McCarthy, Charles McCarthy, Alice Turner, John Turner

**MYSTERY** Holmes goes to Hertfordshire to clear a young man accused of his father's murder; after inspecting the crime scene, all Holmes can deduce is that the murderer is 'a tall man, left-handed, limps with the right leg, wears thick-soled shooting-boots and a grey cloak, smokes Indian cigars, uses a cigarette holder and carries a blunt penknife in his pocket.' Sherlock's knowledge of Australia then enables him to find the real murderer…

## 'The Five Orange Pips'

**FIRST PUBLISHED** *Strand Magazine*, November 1891

**MAJOR PLAYERS** Holmes, Watson, John Openshaw, Elias Openshaw, Joseph Openshaw

**MYSTERY** Sherlock tackles the Ku Klux Klan, as John Openshaw brings him the five orange pips he has received, something that spelled death for his uncle and father. Holmes inexplicably allows him to journey back to Sussex, but he never arrives, and the Great Detective swears revenge on the murderers.

## 'The Man with the Twisted Lip'

**FIRST PUBLISHED** *Strand Magazine*, December 1891

**MAJOR PLAYERS** Holmes, Watson, Hugh Boone, Neville St Clair, Isa Whitney, Mrs St Clair

**MYSTERY** After disguising himself as an opium addict, Sherlock solves the mystery of the disappearance and possible murder of Neville St Clair after an entire night of pondering with his pipe, one of the most intense smoking sessions in any of the stories.

## 'The Adventure of the Blue Carbuncle'

FIRST PUBLISHED *Strand Magazine*, January 1892

MAJOR PLAYERS Holmes, Watson, James Ryder, Henry Baker, Peterson, Mrs Oakshott, Mr Windigate, John Horner

MYSTERY At the beginning of this story Holmes is brought a hat, a goose and, finally, the carbuncle in question, which is a stolen valuable gem discovered hidden in the crop of the Christmas goose. Holmes determines to discover whether the man arrested for the crime, John Horner, is in fact the thief.

## 'The Adventure of the Speckled Band'

FIRST PUBLISHED *Strand Magazine*, February 1892

MAJOR PLAYERS Holmes, Watson, Dr Grimesby Roylott, Helen Stoner, Julia Stoner

MYSTERY Helen Stoner comes to Holmes in fear of her life. She has announced her engagement and fears that she will suffer the same fate as her sister Julia, who died in her arms two years before on the eve of her wedding. Julia's dying words were: 'It was the band! The speckled band!' Holmes and Watson set up vigil in Helen's room and, in the dead of night, save the day. Doyle wrote a hugely successful play based on the story in 1910.

## 'The Adventure of the Engineer's Thumb'

**FIRST PUBLISHED** *Strand Magazine*, March 1892

**MAJOR PLAYERS** Holmes, Watson, Victor Hatherley, Colonel Lysander Stark, Mr Ferguson, Elise, Inspector Bradstreet

**MYSTERY** An engineer called to secretly repair a large pressing machine almost ends up beneath it – he escapes with only the loss of his thumb to a swipe of a meat cleaver, and enlists Sherlock's help to track down the location of where he was so nearly killed.

## 'The Adventure of the Noble Bachelor'

**FIRST PUBLISHED** *Strand Magazine*, April 1892

**MAJOR PLAYERS** Holmes, Watson, Lord St Simon, Hatty Doran, Flora Millar, Francis Hay Moulton

**MYSTERY** Lord St Simon's new wife Hatty disappears immediately after their wedding, and the only crumb of evidence is that she dropped her bouquet and it was picked up for her by a man in the front pew. Inspector Lestrade leaps into action and inevitably arrests the wrong person, leaving Sherlock to rescue the situation.

## 'The Adventure of the Beryl Coronet'

FIRST PUBLISHED *Strand Magazine*, May 1892

MAJOR PLAYERS  Holmes, Watson, Alexander Holder,
Arthur Holder, Sir George Burnwell, Mary Holder, Lucy Parr

MYSTERY  When Alexander Holder is given an immensely
valuable coronet as collateral, he makes the unwise decision
to take it home for safekeeping, then wakes in the night to find
his son apparently tearing apart the coronet – three of its gems
are missing. Holmes is not fooled by the obvious, tracks down
the real villain and recovers the jewels.

## 'The Adventure of the Copper Beeches'

FIRST PUBLISHED  *Strand Magazine*, June 1892

MAJOR PLAYERS  Holmes, Watson, Violet Hunter,
Jephro Rucastle, Alice Rucastle, Mrs Rucastle, Mr Fowler

MYSTERY  Why has a governess been hired to have her hair
cut, wear a blue dress and sit in a chair facing a window
listening to funny stories? Sherlock sees through the mystery,
and Watson shoots a dog.

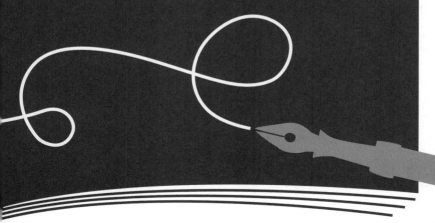

# A POLICEMAN'S LOT

Though a great respecter of the law, there are very few members of the police force that Sherlock Holmes has any time for. Here is a collection of his dismissals, sarcastic remarks and insults.

*'Lestrade, I congratulate you! With your usual happy mixture of cunning and audacity you have got him.'*
*'Got him! Got whom, Mr Holmes?'*
'THE EMPTY HOUSE'

*When Gregson or Lestrade or Athelney Jones are out of their depths — which, by the way, is their normal state ...*
THE SIGN OF FOUR

*It is just in such details that the skilled detective differs from the Gregson and Lestrade type.*
A STUDY IN SCARLET

*...that imbecile Lestrade ...*
'THE BOSCOMBE VALLEY MYSTERY'

48

'By George!' cried the inspector.
'How did you ever see that?'
'Because I looked for it.'

'THE DANCING MEN'

'Ha! I have a theory. These flashes
come upon me at times ... What
do you think of this, Holmes?
... The brother died in a fit, on
which Sholto walked off with
the treasure! How's that?'

'On which the dead man
very considerately got up
and locked the door on the
inside,' said Holmes.

THE SIGN OF FOUR

I understand, however,
from the inquest that
there were some objects
which you failed to
overlook.

'BLACK PETER'

# BAKER STREET IRREGULARS

This group of street urchins – 'the Baker Street division of the detective police force', as Holmes calls them in *The Sign of Four* – was recruited by the detective to perform various missions, generally to search London following clues and to go to places where Sherlock himself could not. Watson first encounters them in *A Study in Scarlet* and describes their appearance: 'six dirty little scoundrels stood in line like so many disreputable statuettes'. Their chief was the energetic and inventive Wiggins. Holmes explained to Watson that their very ordinariness allowed them to 'go everywhere and see everything. They are as sharp as needles, too.' He paid them well: a shilling a day plus expenses, with a guinea bonus for whoever found the object of their search.

## CASES INVOLVING THE IRREGULARS

As with Moriarty and Mycroft, the Irregulars have exerted an influence on the legacy of Sherlock Holmes out of proportion to their appearances in the original stories.

| STORY | ROLE |
|---|---|
| A STUDY IN SCARLET | Finding the cab driven by Jefferson Hope |
| THE SIGN OF FOUR | Finding the steam launch *Aurora* |
| 'THE CROOKED MAN' | Watching over Henry Wood |

In 1934 a Baker Street Irregulars society was founded in New York devoted to the study and appreciation of Sherlock Holmes. Their arcane by-laws, which contain several references to the 'Sacred Writings', conclude:

*(4) All other business shall be left for the monthly meeting.*

*(5) There shall be no monthly meeting.*

# HOLMES vs WOMEN

Sherlock was not a devotee of the female sex, and – presumably with the exception of when he became engaged to aid an investigation ('Charles Augustus Milverton') – he seldom bothered to hide his feelings.

*Women are never to be entirely trusted – not the best of them.*

THE SIGN OF FOUR

*[Holmes] disliked and distrusted the sex, but he was always a chivalrous opponent.*

'THE DYING DETECTIVE'

*Their most trivial action may mean volumes, or their most extraordinary conduct may depend upon a hairpin or a curling tongs.*

'THE SECOND STAIN'

*I am not a whole-souled admirer of woman-kind.*

THE VALLEY OF FEAR

*Woman's heart and mind are insoluble puzzles to the male.*

'THE ILLUSTRIOUS CLIENT'

However, he was not averse to paying them the occasional back-handed compliment:

*The impression of a woman may be more valuable than the conclusion of an analytical reasoner.*

'THE MAN WITH THE TWISTED LIP'

# THE MEMOIRS OF SHERLOCK HOLMES

The second collection of Sherlock Holmes cases was published in 1894. 'The Adventure of the Cardboard Box', with its treatment of adultery, caused some unease at the time and was subsequently left out of many editions of *Memoirs*. It was later included in the collection *His Last Bow* (1917).

## 'Silver Blaze'

**FIRST PUBLISHED** *Strand Magazine*, December 1892

**MAJOR PLAYERS** Holmes, Watson, Colonel Ross, Inspector Gregory, John Straker

**MYSTERY** Silver Blaze, favourite for the Wessex Cup, has disappeared from its stable, and the trainer has been found dead, killed by a wicked blow to the head. The obvious suspect, a racing tout, is arrested. Holmes travels to Devon, and not only solves the case but returns Silver Blaze in time for it to win the Cup.

## 'The Adventure of the Cardboard Box'

**FIRST PUBLISHED** *Strand Magazine*, January 1893

**MAJOR PLAYERS** Holmes, Watson, Susan Cushing, Mary Cushing, Lestrade, Sarah Cushing, James Browner

MYSTERY A gruesome case in which a woman, Susan Cushing, receives a box containing two human ears packed in salt. Holmes, who is of course an expert on ears, eventually untangles this unpleasant case of murder and adultery revolving around three sisters and one man.

## 'The Adventure of the Yellow Face'

FIRST PUBLISHED *Strand Magazine*, February 1893

MAJOR PLAYERS Holmes, Watson, Grant Munro, Effie Munro

MYSTERY One of Sherlock's few investigations that ends in complete failure. Grant Munro reports his wife's unusual behaviour, asking for £100 (of her own money!) and paying visits at odd hours to a neighbouring cottage from which a 'yellow livid face' has been seen peering. Even Holmes suspects wrongdoing – he forms an opinion, sticks to it, and is proved utterly wrong.

## 'The Adventure of the Stockbroker's Clerk'

FIRST PUBLISHED *Strand Magazine*, March 1893

MAJOR PLAYERS Holmes, Watson, Hall Pycroft, Arthur Pinner, Harry Pinner

MYSTERY Hall Pycroft is interviewed by two brothers, one in London and one in Birmingham – it seems evident to him that the brothers are one and the same person, and the puzzle leads him to consult Sherlock Holmes, who heads to the Midlands to solve the case.

## 'The Adventure of the Gloria Scott'

**FIRST PUBLISHED** *Strand Magazine*, April 1893

**MAJOR PLAYERS** Holmes, Watson, Victor Trevor Jr, Victor Trevor Sr, Beddoes, Hudson

**MYSTERY** Sherlock's very first case, solved while he was still at college. A cryptic message strikes a JP dead with terror when he reads it: 'The supply of game for London is going steadily up. Head keeper Hudson, we believe, has been now told to receive all orders for fly-paper and for preservation of your hen pheasant's life.' Sherlock cracks the riddle and solves a decades-old mystery.

## 'The Adventure of the Musgrave Ritual'

**FIRST PUBLISHED** *Strand Magazine*, May 1893

**MAJOR PLAYERS** Holmes, Reginald Musgrave, Brunton, Rachel Howells, Janet Tregellis

**MYSTERY** The Musgrave Ritual refers to an arcane rite recited by members of the Musgrave family. Now Brunton the butler has disappeared without a trace. Sherlock's relics of the case comprise a crumpled piece of paper, a brass key, a peg of wood with a ball of string attached and three rusty old discs of metal. This story is unusual in that, after a short introduction from Watson, it is related entirely by Holmes.

## 'The Adventure of the Reigate Squires'

**FIRST PUBLISHED** *Strand Magazine*, June 1893

**MAJOR PLAYERS** Holmes, Watson, Colonel Hayter,
William Kirwin, Cunningham, Alec Cunningham

**MYSTERY** Holmes has been overworking, so Watson takes
him to the country to stay with an old army acquaintance,
Colonel Hayter. While there, a series of burglaries culminates
in the murder of Kirwin the coachman. Holmes uses his
expertise in handwriting to solve the crime.

## 'The Adventure of the Crooked Man'

**FIRST PUBLISHED** *Strand Magazine*, July 1893

**MAJOR PLAYERS** Holmes, Watson, Nancy Barclay,
Colonel Barclay, Henry Wood

**MYSTERY** Colonel Barclay has been found dead in a pool
of blood with his wife in an apparent coma beside him – an
argument between them was overheard. Holmes soon deduces
that there was another person in the room, and a small
creature that expressed a culinary interest in a caged canary.
The 'Crooked Man' is soon discovered.

## 'The Adventure of the Resident Patient'

FIRST PUBLISHED *Strand Magazine*, August 1893

MAJOR PLAYERS Holmes, Watson, Percy Trevelyan,
Mr Blessington, Worthingdon Bank Gang

MYSTERY A young doctor, Trevelyan, is set up in practice
by a wealthy sponsor, Blessington. But Blessington's recent
agitated actions cause Trevelyan to consult Holmes. He
confronts Blessington, to no effect, and the next morning the
man is found hanged in his room. Sherlock's brilliant analysis
of the room allows him to formulate a remarkably clear picture
of what happened.

## 'The Adventure of the Greek Interpreter'

FIRST PUBLISHED *Strand Magazine*, September 1893

MAJOR PLAYERS Holmes, Watson, Mycroft Holmes, Mr Melas,
Paul Kratides, Sophy Kratides, Wilson Kemp, Harold Latimer

MYSTERY A case notable for what we learn of Mycroft
Holmes, it revolves around the abduction of a professional
Greek interpreter, who is forced to translate demands to
another captive, Paul Kratides. As a diversion, there is a
delightful deductive tussle between Sherlock and Mycroft
over an old soldier they observe from the Diogenes Club.

## 'The Adventure of the Naval Treaty'

FIRST PUBLISHED *Strand Magazine*, October and November 1893

MAJOR PLAYERS Holmes, Watson, Percy Phelps,
Annie Harrison, Joseph Harrison, Forbes, Mrs Tangey

MYSTERY A long story originally published in two parts, it
concerns a schoolmate of Watson's, now at the Foreign Office,
who has an important document stolen from his desk, but no
demands or repercussions have been forthcoming in the two
months since it disappeared. Holmes successfully retrieves the
papers, remarking the case was 'certainly one of the darkest
which I have ever investigated'.

## 'The Final Problem'

FIRST PUBLISHED *Strand Magazine*, December 1893

MAJOR PLAYERS Holmes, Watson, Professor Moriarty,
Peter Steiler

MYSTERY Perhaps not even Sherlock Holmes himself could
have predicted the outcry this killing off of a character that
had gripped the world's attention would cause. Holmes has
set everything in place to destroy the web of crime woven by
Professor Moriarty, but must flee to the Continent for his own
safety. The inevitable confrontation, however, takes place in
Switzerland at the Reichenbach Falls. Watson noted, 'Any
attempt at recovering the bodies was absolutely hopeless…'

# HOLMES LETS THEM OFF

Despite his admiration for the law, Holmes observes to Watson in 'The Abbey Grange': 'Once or twice in my career I feel that I have done more real harm by my discovery of the criminal than ever he had done by his crime ... I had rather play tricks with the law of England than with my own conscience.'

It should come as no surprise, therefore, that there are several occasions in his investigating career where, for various reasons – mercy, sympathy, national interest – Holmes uses his discretion and turns a blind eye.

| CASE | CRIMINAL |
|---|---|
| 'The Blue Carbuncle' | James Ryder |
| 'The Boscombe Valley Mystery' | John Turner |
| 'The Naval Treaty' | Joseph Harrison |
| 'The Devil's Foot' | Leon Sterndale |
| 'The Abbey Grange' | Jack Croker |
| 'The Veiled Lodger' | Eugenia Ronder |

## CRIME

Theft

Murder

Theft

Murder

Murder

Conspiracy to murder

# THE REICHENBACH FALLS

Second to 221B Baker Street, this is the most famous site in all of the stories, for it was here that Holmes apparently met his demise at the hands of Professor Moriarty in 'The Final Problem'. Holmes, based on Watson's deductions, entered into his struggles with the evil professor on the ledge overlooking the falls, as depicted in Sidney Paget's famous illustration.

The Falls are a series of cataracts situated along the Reichenbach River in central Switzerland near the village of Meiringen, and have a total drop of 250 metres. Doyle was apparently shown the falls by Sir Henry Lunn, the founder of the travel company Lunn Poly.

## COMMEMORATION

A plaque on the ledge marks the spot, with an inscription in English, German and French pronouncing: 'At this fearful place, Sherlock Holmes vanquished Professor Moriarty, on 4 May 1891'. The plaque was erected by two Sherlock appreciation societies, The Bimetallic Question of Montreal and The Reichenbach Irregulars of Switzerland.

## MEIRINGEN

As well as being famous for its Sherlock connection, Meiringen also claims to be the birthplace of the meringue, although this is disputed. What is not disputed is the influence of the Great Detective on the town, which has its own Sherlock Holmes Museum complete with a life-size Holmes statue outside it. The statue and accompanying plaques contain 60 clues, one for each of the Conan Doyle stories.

PLACE

# HOLMES THE MATHEMATICIAN

Sherlock's gift for mental arithmetic is demonstrated more than once in the stories (although when Watson calls him a 'calculating-machine', it is more a general observation than a mathematical one). In 'Silver Blaze' he works out the speed of the train – 'fifty three and a half miles an hour' – not by using quarter-mile posts (which would be impressive enough) but by the telegraph posts, which 'upon this line are sixty yards apart – the calculation is a simple one'. He also has no problem working out the problem of 'The Musgrave Ritual', which calls for a little knowledge of geometry. And in *A Study in Scarlet* he remarks to Watson: 'the height of a man, in nine cases out of ten, can be told from the length of his stride. It is a simple calculation enough, though there is no use my boring you with figures.'

But perhaps Conan Doyle also had a fascination with maths and mathematicians. Among the characters he introduces are:

## PROFESSOR MORIARTY

A maths genius who wrote a treatise upon the binomial theorem aged 21, became a maths professor soon afterwards, and wrote *The Dynamics of an Asteroid*, described by Holmes as 'a book which ascends to such rarefied heights of pure mathematics that it is said that there was no man in the scientific press capable of criticising it'.

## AVELING

A mathematics master at the school in 'The Priory School'.

## IAN MURDOCH

A maths tutor at The Gables in 'The Lion's Mane'.

# INSPECTOR LESTRADE

An inspector of Scotland Yard and the most well-known policeman in the stories, Lestrade first appeared in *A Study in Scarlet* looking into the murder of Enoch Drebber, competing with Inspector Gregson to solve the mystery. Holmes noted the pair's rivalry: 'They have their knives into one another.' Despite his best efforts to impress Holmes, even when he finds the vital piece of evidence in the form of a note scribbled on the back of a hotel receipt ('A Noble Bachelor'), it transpires he should have been looking at the receipt, not the note.

Whatever his deficiencies, he must have had a good PR man, as whenever he is mentioned in the press it is always in glowing terms: 'one of the very smartest of our detective officers' ('The Cardboard Box'). And he must have been on reasonably good terms with Dr Watson at least, who informs us in *A Study in Scarlet* that he has had access to Lestrade's notebook. Perhaps the policeman would have refused this request if he knew Watson had referred to him, at various times and in descending order of desirability, as dapper, wiry, thin, austere, ferret-like and rat-faced.

The clumsy copper has featured frequently in spin-offs, spoofs and parodies, often having Sherlock's admittedly low opinion of him exaggerated for comic effect. This reached absurd heights with the characterisation of Lestrade in the Basil Rathbone films in which the inspector was portrayed as a complete idiot by Dennis Hoey. Other films have attempted to treat him more fairly, notably Frank Finlay in *Murder by Decree* (1979), and Rupert Graves gives a sympathetic rendition of him in BBC TV's *Sherlock*, where we even discover he has a first name – Greg.

**FAMOUS PORTRAYALS OF LESTRADE**

**DENNIS HOEY**

SIX FILMS FROM 1942–46

**BILL OWEN**

SHERLOCK HOLMES (TV, 1951)

# TEN OF LESTRADE'S SCOTLAND YARD COLLEAGUES

**Although Lestrade is the most famous of the policemen who are assisted and insulted by Holmes, he is by no means the only one.**

**1** INSPECTOR BRADSTREET ('The Man with the Twisted Lip', 'The Blue Carbuncle', 'The Engineer's Thumb')

**2** FORBES ('The Naval Treaty')

**3** INSPECTOR GREGSON (*A Study in Scarlet*, *The Sign of Four*, 'The Greek Interpreter', 'The Red Circle', 'Wisteria Lodge')

**4** STANLEY HOPKINS ('The Abbey Grange', 'Black Peter', 'The Golden Pince-Nez')

**5** ATHELNEY JONES (*The Sign of Four*)

**6** INSPECTOR PETER JONES ('The Red-Headed League')

**7** INSPECTOR ALEC MACDONALD (*The Valley of Fear*)

**8** INSPECTOR MACKINNON ('The Retired Colourman')

**9** INSPECTOR MONTGOMERY ('The Cardboard Box')

**10** INSPECTOR MORTON ('The Dying Detective')

**FRANK FINLAY**
A STUDY IN TERROR (1965), MURDER BY DECREE (1979)

**RUPERT GRAVES**
SHERLOCK, BBC TV, (2010–)

**SEAN PERTWEE**
ELEMENTARY, CBS TV (2012–)

# CLUBS AND RESTAURANTS

Despite being so unclubbable that he is an admirer (if not an actual member) of the Diogenes Club, several other gentlemen's establishments are mentioned in the stories.

| CLUB | NOTABLE MEMBERS |
| --- | --- |
| Anglo-Indian | Colonel Sebastian Moran |
| Bagatelle | Colonel Sebastian Moran<br>Ronald Adair |
| Baldwin | Ronald Adair |
| Carlton | Sir James Damery |
| Cavendish | Ronald Adair |
| Tankerville | Colonel Sebastian Moran<br>Major Prendergast |

Holmes doesn't seem to be a great social entertainer. The one time in the stories he invites Watson for a meal, the message runs as follows:

*Am dining at Goldini's Restaurant, Gloucester Road, Kensington. Please come at once and join me there. Bring with you a jemmy, a dark lantern, a chisel and a revolver.*

'THE BRUCE-PARTINGTON PLANS'

## CASES

'The Empty House'

'The Empty House'

'The Empty House'

'The Illustrious Client'

'The Empty House'

'The Empty House' and 'The Five Orange Pips'

# THE HOUND OF THE BASKER-VILLES

## FIRST PUBLISHED

*Strand Magazine*, August 1901–April 1902; published as a novel 1902

## MAJOR PLAYERS

Holmes, Watson, Sir Henry Baskerville, Dr Mortimer, Jack Stapleton, Beryl Stapleton

# MYSTERY

The most famous, most popular and generally considered the best written of all the accounts of Dr Watson, containing elements of the supernatural, the Gothic and the classic detective novel.

Holmes is too busy to attend personally to the case brought to him by Dr Mortimer; he sends Watson to Baskerville Hall on Dartmoor as his surrogate. When Holmes finally makes his dramatic appearance, the doctor is praised for once for his good work. The case itself, involving the murder of Sir Charles Baskerville, the attempted murder of his nephew and heir Sir Henry, and the apparent return of the dreaded hound that curses the Baskervilles, is one of the darkest of the detective's career, made particularly so by the skill and cunning of his vicious opponent. The forbidding Grimpen Mire is a fitting location for the grim conclusion of the story.

During its run in *Strand*, the story increased the magazine's circulation by some 30,000 copies, devoured by a public desperate for the return of the Great Detective.

# SHERLOCK BY NUMBERS

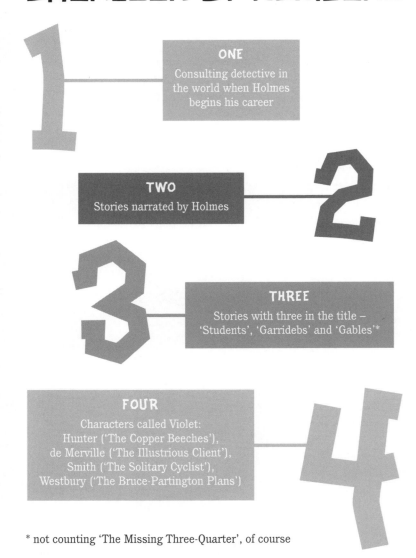

**ONE**
Consulting detective in the world when Holmes begins his career

**TWO**
Stories narrated by Holmes

**THREE**
Stories with three in the title –
'Students', 'Garridebs' and 'Gables'*

**FOUR**
Characters called Violet:
Hunter ('The Copper Beeches'),
de Merville ('The Illustrious Client'),
Smith ('The Solitary Cyclist'),
Westbury ('The Bruce-Partington Plans')

* not counting 'The Missing Three-Quarter', of course

## FIVE

Pillows sat on by Holmes while he consumed an ounce of shag in order to solve the case of 'The Man with the Twisted Lip'

## SIX

Members of the Baker Street Irregulars that assemble in Holmes' room in *A Study in Scarlet*

## SEVEN

Mud-spatters Holmes counts on Helen Stoner's jacket in 'The Speckled Band'

## EIGHT

Weeks Jabez Wilson spends copying out the encyclopedia in 'The Red-Headed League'

## NINE

Weeks of 'brain-fever' suffered by Percy Phelps after the Naval Treaty goes missing from his office

## TEN

Minutes of silence before Munro does the decent thing in 'The Yellow Face'

# DR JOHN WATSON

## LIFE BEFORE HOLMES

Despite the faithful and modest Watson's reluctance to discuss himself, references made throughout the stories paint a fairly clear picture of his life.

Born somewhere in the early 1850s, he spent his early life in Australia before returning to England to go to school. He entered the University of London Medical School, and probably played rugby for Blackheath at around this time. After his medical studies he became an army surgeon stationed in India when the Second Afghan War broke out. Watson was wounded at the Battle of Maiwand in 1880. While recovering from his wound he contracted enteric fever, which nearly killed him, and he was finally sent back to England.

He was looking for cheap lodgings when he bumped into an old friend from Bart's hospital. He was able to put Watson in touch with an eccentric young man called Sherlock Holmes.

## THE ODD COUPLE

Considering his rather odd habits, one pities anyone who had to live with Holmes: Watson somehow managed it for well over a decade in total, firstly from 1881 until his first marriage in 1886 or 1887, then from late 1888 (after the death of his wife) until he married Mary Morstan in May 1889, and finally from 1894 (when Holmes came back to life and by which time poor Mary had also died) until 1902. In the recent BBC TV series *Sherlock* much is made of the relationship between the two men, with other characters (notably Mrs Hudson) frequently assuming, much to Watson's frustration, that they must be gay.

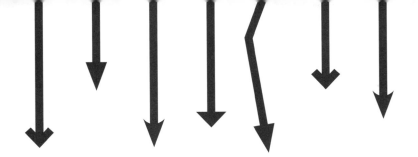

## WATSON THE LOVER

Of course, as Doyle's stories make it clear, Watson is quite a ladies' man. 'The fair sex is your department,' Holmes observes in 'The Second Stain'. He seems to have been married at least three times, though only the name of the second, Mary Morstan, is known. Let us hope the third Mrs Watson was luckier than the first two, who both died within a few years of their weddings.

## WATSON AND HOLMES

As is the case with any personal relationship, the long association of sleuth and sidekick underwent inevitable and gradual changes. Their early years together were quite harmonious and Watson noted in 'The Five Orange Pips' that he was the only friend of the detective. After Watson's marriage (or marriages) they drifted apart, as noted in 'A Scandal in Bohemia'.

Holmes' return from Reichenbach to a widowed Watson brought them together again for many an adventure. Sherlock's cold and logical demeanour often seemed to disappoint Watson, so when the doctor is shot in 'The Three Garridebs' the worried reaction of the Great Detective to his friend's condition is immensely gratifying to him. Sherlock tells the assailant that if he had killed Watson he would not have left the room alive. Watson observes, 'It was worth a wound – it was worth many wounds – to know the depth of loyalty and love which lay behind that cold mask.'

Although they went their separate ways after Sherlock's retirement in 1903 and Watson's (final?) remarriage, when it came time to wrap up the spymaster Von Bork in 1914, it was unthinkable to Holmes to go into danger without the friend who had shared in his adventures so faithfully and for so long.

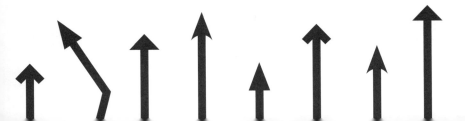

## WITH FRIENDS LIKE THESE...

No wonder Watson was gratified to hear the occasional word of praise or affection from Holmes. The opposite was much more often the case.

> You see, but you do not observe. The distinction is clear.
>
> 'A SCANDAL IN BOHEMIA'

> A very pretty hash you have made of it ... I cannot at the moment consider any possible blunder you have omitted.
>
> 'THE DISAPPEARANCE OF LADY FRANCES CARFAX'

> Your hiding place, my dear Watson, was very faulty ... you really have done remarkably badly.
>
> 'THE SOLITARY CYCLIST'

> Watson. Come at once if convenient — if inconvenient come all the same.
>
> 'THE CREEPING MAN'

> 'Pon my word, Watson, you are coming along wonderfully. You have really done very well indeed. It is true that you have missed everything of importance...
>
> 'A CASE OF IDENTITY'

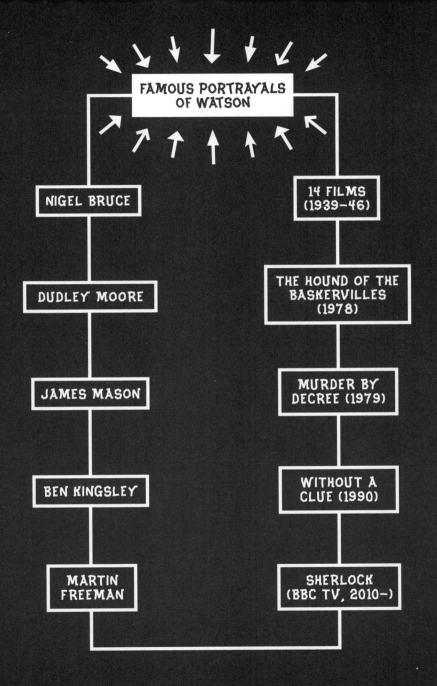

FAMOUS PORTRAYALS
OF WATSON

NIGEL BRUCE

DUDLEY MOORE

JAMES MASON

BEN KINGSLEY

MARTIN
FREEMAN

14 FILMS
(1939–46)

THE HOUND OF THE
BASKERVILLES
(1978)

MURDER BY
DECREE (1979)

WITHOUT A
CLUE (1990)

SHERLOCK
(BBC TV, 2010–)

# SHERLOCK HOLMES ON THE RADIO

| DATE | PROGRAMME OR SERIES |
|------|---------------------|
| 1930 | 'The Adventure of the Speckled Band' |
| 1939–47 | *The Adventures of Sherlock Holmes*<br>*Sherlock Holmes*<br>*The New Adventures of Sherlock Holmes* |
| 1954 | 'The Adventures of Sherlock Holmes' |
| 1953–69 | Various Sherlock adventures |
| 1989–98 | The Complete Series (all 60 stories) |

As has often been said, 'You get better pictures on the radio.' Whether or not that's true, you can certainly create an abundance of scenes and effects for a fraction of the budget (no messing around with CGI hounds), and Sherlock Holmes has been a staple of radio drama almost since the medium was invented. Here are a few of the most famous and/or long-running.

| COUNTRY | HOLMES & WATSON |
|---------|-----------------|
| US | William Gillette and Leigh Lovell |
| US | Basil Rathbone and Nigel Bruce |
| UK | John Gielgud and Ralph Richardson |
| UK | Carleton Hobbs and Norman Shelley |
| UK | Clive Merrison and Michael Williams |

# SHERLOCK TRIVIA

Sherlock Holmes suffered from rheumatism in old age.

In both 'The Five Orange Pips' and 'The Resident Patient' the murderers escape British justice only to be lost at sea.

Sherlock Holmes once gave an innocent dog a pill he suspected to be poisoned (it was).

Moriarty is the only character in the Sherlock Holmes films to have been killed off three times in the same series (the Basil Rathbone movies). All involved him falling from a great height.

Sherlock Holmes can distinguish between 75 different perfumes.

Altamont, Sherlock's alias in 'His Last Bow', was the middle name of Doyle's father.

Sherlock Holmes enjoyed the music of renaissance composer Orlandus Lassus.

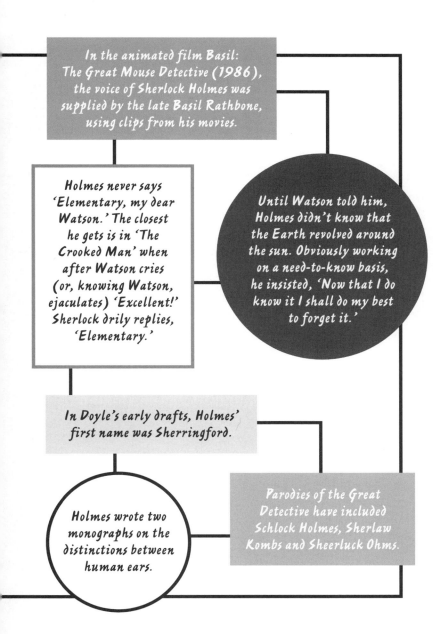

In the animated film Basil: The Great Mouse Detective (1986), the voice of Sherlock Holmes was supplied by the late Basil Rathbone, using clips from his movies.

Holmes never says 'Elementary, my dear Watson.' The closest he gets is in 'The Crooked Man' when after Watson cries (or, knowing Watson, ejaculates) 'Excellent!' Sherlock drily replies, 'Elementary.'

Until Watson told him, Holmes didn't know that the Earth revolved around the sun. Obviously working on a need-to-know basis, he insisted, 'Now that I do know it I shall do my best to forget it.'

In Doyle's early drafts, Holmes' first name was Sherringford.

Holmes wrote two monographs on the distinctions between human ears.

Parodies of the Great Detective have included Schlock Holmes, Sherlaw Kombs and Sheerluck Ohms.

# THE RETURN OF SHERLOCK HOLMES

The third collection of short stories, published in book form in 1908, featured those adventures that were released following Sherlock's triumphant return in 1894 after what became known as the 'Great Hiatus'.

## 'The Adventure of the Empty House'

**FIRST PUBLISHED** *Strand Magazine*, October 1903

**MAJOR PLAYERS** Holmes, Watson, Ronald Adair, Lestrade, Colonel Sebastian Moran, Mrs Hudson

**MYSTERY** Three years after the tussle at Reichenbach, Watson is still bereft, having also lost his beloved wife Mary. London is abuzz with the bizarre murder of Ronald Adair, shot at close range in a locked room. Watson attempts to apply his late friend's methods (and you can guess how successful he is). In the midst of this darkness Holmes suddenly returns, causing Watson to faint. With the help of Mrs Hudson, they set about finding Adair's killer.

## 'The Adventure of the Norwood Builder'

**FIRST PUBLISHED** *Strand Magazine*, November 1903

**MAJOR PLAYERS** Holmes, Watson, John Hector McFarlane, Lestrade, Jonas Oldacre, Mrs Lexington

**MYSTERY** John McFarlane is arrested for the murder of Jonas Oldacre, after some burned remains are found at Oldacre's house. McFarlane had been at the house drawing up a will that left all Oldacre's estate to him. When the bloody thumbprint of the young solicitor is found upon a wall, it looks even worse for him. Sherlock solves the case with the help of wet straw, a bucket of water and several constables with good loud voices.

## 'The Adventure of the Dancing Men'

**FIRST PUBLISHED** *Strand Magazine*, December 1903

**MAJOR PLAYERS** Holmes, Watson, Hilton Cubitt, Elsie Cubitt, Abe Slaney

**MYSTERY** A mystery with a code is always an enticing teaser, and the appearance of the dancing men that have agitated Elsie Cubitt so much was a favourite of the author. What seems merely a puzzle takes a grim turn when Hilton and Elsie Cubitt are found shot (and Hilton dead) in what appears at first to be a murder-suicide – or will be if Elsie dies of her wounds. By cracking the code, Holmes solves the case.

## 'The Adventure of the Solitary Cyclist'

**FIRST PUBLISHED** *Strand Magazine*, January 1904

**MAJOR PLAYERS** Holmes, Watson, Violet Smith, Robert Carruthers, Jack Woodley

**MYSTERY** Holmes sends Watson to look into this case, where a young lady is followed by a bearded man on a bicycle. The Great Detective is soon forced to take over, but not quickly enough to prevent a near tragedy.

## 'The Adventure of the Priory School'

**FIRST PUBLISHED** *Strand Magazine*, February 1904

**MAJOR PLAYERS** Holmes, Watson, Dr Thorneycroft Huxtable, Lord Saltire, Heidegger, Reuben Hayes, James Wilder

**MYSTERY** The disappearance of a titled 10-year-old schoolboy from his prep school brings the headmaster to Baker Street in desperation. The school's German master has also disappeared, and is later found dead with his head bashed in. The major clue is a set of cycle tracks that (supposedly) enable Sherlock to deduce the direction of travel. One of the few instances where Holmes accepts a large fee for his work.

## 'The Adventure of Black Peter'

**FIRST PUBLISHED** *Strand Magazine*, March 1904

**MAJOR PLAYERS** Holmes, Watson, Inspector Hopkins, John Hopley Neligan, Captain Peter Carey, Patrick Cairns

**MYSTERY** 'Black Peter', aka Captain Carey, is found impaled on a wall by a harpoon in the garden of his retirement home. Inspector Hopkins arrests John Neligan, but Holmes, at the top of his form according to Watson, has his doubts. He enlists 'Captain Basil', an Arctic explorer, to help him find the real killer.

## 'The Adventure of Charles Augustus Milverton'

FIRST PUBLISHED *Strand Magazine*, April 1904

MAJOR PLAYERS Holmes, Watson, Milverton, Lestrade

MYSTERY Holmes is pitched against Milverton, the 'king of all the blackmailers'. Engaged to recover some incriminating letters, Sherlock takes the morally dubious route of becoming engaged to Milverton's housemaid. The case concludes with tragic and bloody events.

## 'The Adventure of the Six Napoleons'

FIRST PUBLISHED *Strand Magazine*, May 1904

MAJOR PLAYERS Holmes, Watson, Lestrade, Beppo, Horace Harker

MYSTERY Someone is going round London smashing busts of Napoleon Bonaparte – hardly a sinister happening, until the body of Mafia thug Pietro Venucci turns up on the doorstep of one of the bust-owners. Holmes reveals the truth with such stunning legerdemain and panache that he gets a round of applause from Watson and Lestrade.

## 'The Adventure of the Three Students'

FIRST PUBLISHED *Strand Magazine*, June 1904

MAJOR PLAYERS Holmes, Watson, Hilton Soames, Gilchrist, Daulat Ras, Miles McLaren, Bannister

MYSTERY One of the three competing students for the prestigious Fortescue Scholarship has attempted to cheat by looking at the test in advance. But which one? Vital clues include three lumps of black, doughy clay, shavings and gloves.

## 'The Adventure of the Golden Pince-Nez'

**FIRST PUBLISHED** *Strand Magazine*, July 1904

**MAJOR PLAYERS** Holmes, Watson, Professor Coram, Anna Coram, Mortimer, Mrs Marker, Susan Tarlton

**MYSTERY** Holmes is summoned to Kent to look into the murder of Willoughby Smith, secretary to the invalid Professor Coram. Sherlock's chain-smoking of Alexandrian cigarettes while throwing the ashes on the floor proves critical to the solution. He also performs a brilliant bit of deduction on a pair of spectacles, deriving no fewer than eight pieces of information about the murderer.

## 'The Adventure of the Missing Three-Quarter'

**FIRST PUBLISHED** *Strand Magazine*, August 1904

**MAJOR PLAYERS** Holmes, Watson, Cyril Overton, Lord Mount-James, Dr Leslie Armstrong, Godfrey Staunton, Pompey

**MYSTERY** Godfrey Staunton, star of the Cambridge rugby team, has gone missing and his team-mates now face defeat at the hands of Oxford. Sherlock's search is impeded by the impressive Dr Armstrong at every turn, but he finally tracks Staunton down with the help of Pompey, 'pride of the local draghounds' ... too late, alas, to save Cambridge in the match.

## 'The Adventure of the Abbey Grange'

**FIRST PUBLISHED** *Strand Magazine*, September 1904

**MAJOR PLAYERS** Holmes, Watson, Mary Brackenstall, Captain Jack Croker, Theresa, Sir Eustace Brackenstall, Inspector Stanley Hopkins

**MYSTERY** Sir Eustace Brackenstall has been brutally murdered, apparently by burglars. The prime suspects are the Randall Gang. The case proves much more complex, and in the end Holmes demonstrates not only his skills as a detective but his sense of justice.

## 'The Adventure of the Second Stain'

**FIRST PUBLISHED** *Strand Magazine*, December 1904

**MAJOR PLAYERS** Holmes, Watson, Lord Bellinger, Trelawney Hope, Eduardo Lucas, Lady Hilda Trelawney Hope

**MYSTERY** Another case of a stolen government document. One of the suspects, the foreign agent Lucas, is murdered, and an out-of-place 'second blood stain' complicates matters. Nevertheless, Holmes succeeds brilliantly in solving the case and averting disaster.

# MRS HUDSON

The long-suffering landlady of 221B Baker Street was never even given a first name by Doyle. (There has been speculation that Mrs Hudson is Holmes's agent Martha in the household of the German spy in 'His Last Bow', but quite why the author would use her in a story set in 1914 and fail to have either Holmes or Watson refer to her at any time as 'Mrs Hudson' as they have been doing since 1890 seems a mystery Holmes himself would find challenging.) She first appears 'with a crisp knock' in *The Sign of Four* and introduces Miss Mary Morstan, who will eventually become Mrs John Watson.

Over the following years Mrs Hudson has to put up with a constant flow of puzzled and put-upon individuals seeking Holmes's services, as well as the great detective's peculiar habits, such as practising his shooting indoors and his 'weird and often malodorous scientific experiments' ('The Dying Detective'). She probably found the 'princely payments' Holmes made for his rooms sufficient compensation, and seems to have developed a genuine affection for Sherlock – when he returned from the dead in 'The Empty House' she had 'violent hysterics'. This story also showcases Mrs Hudson's finest hour, however, as she rose above the mundanities of years of answering the door, showing in guests and preparing hearty breakfasts to perform the vital task of crawling on her hands and knees in Sherlock's study to turn his wax bust every 15 minutes in order to make it look as if he was sitting in the window.

## IN SHERLOCK'S WORDS

'Her cuisine is a little limited, but she has as good an idea of breakfast as a Scotch-woman.' ('The Naval Treaty')

'Mrs Hudson has been knocked up.' ('The Speckled Band')

## SO GOOD HE NAMED IT ... FOUR TIMES?

Quite why Conan Doyle was so taken with the name we shall never know, but in addition to the Baker Street landlady, Hudson is the name given to the shipwreck survivor turned blackmailer in 'The Gloria Scott', an art-shop owner in 'The Six Napoleons', an unknown man's name in a cryptic message in 'The Five Orange Pips', and even a street name in 'The Crooked Man'.

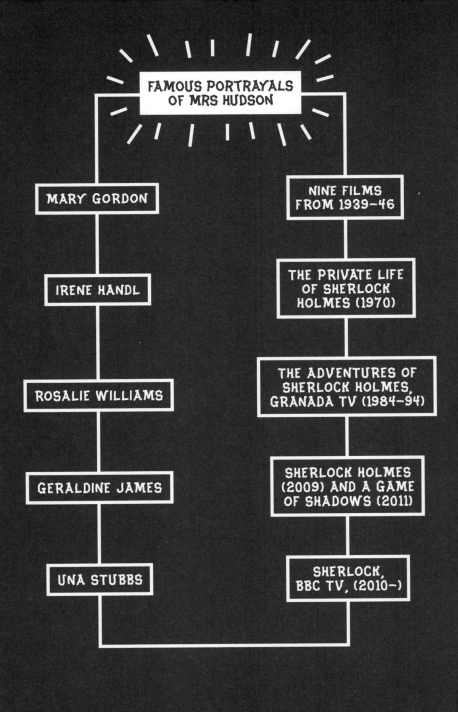

FAMOUS PORTRAYALS
OF MRS HUDSON

MARY GORDON

IRENE HANDL

ROSALIE WILLIAMS

GERALDINE JAMES

UNA STUBBS

NINE FILMS
FROM 1939-46

THE PRIVATE LIFE
OF SHERLOCK
HOLMES (1970)

THE ADVENTURES OF
SHERLOCK HOLMES,
GRANADA TV (1984-94)

SHERLOCK HOLMES
(2009) AND A GAME
OF SHADOWS (2011)

SHERLOCK,
BBC TV, (2010-)

# AN ABC OF SHERLOCK'S SKILLS

Not content with being a world-famous detective with acute observational and deductive powers, and without troubling the remaining 23 letters of the alphabet, Holmes ranges from proficiency to expertise in the following areas:

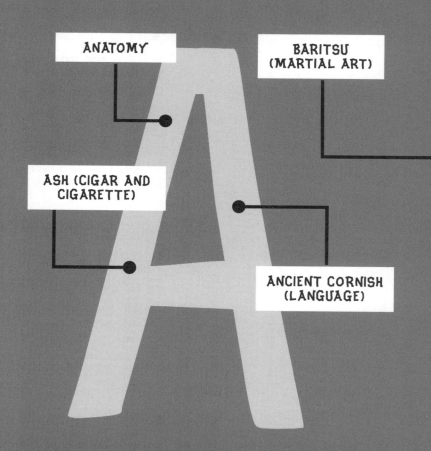

ANATOMY

BARITSU
(MARTIAL ART)

ASH (CIGAR AND
CIGARETTE)

ANCIENT CORNISH
(LANGUAGE)

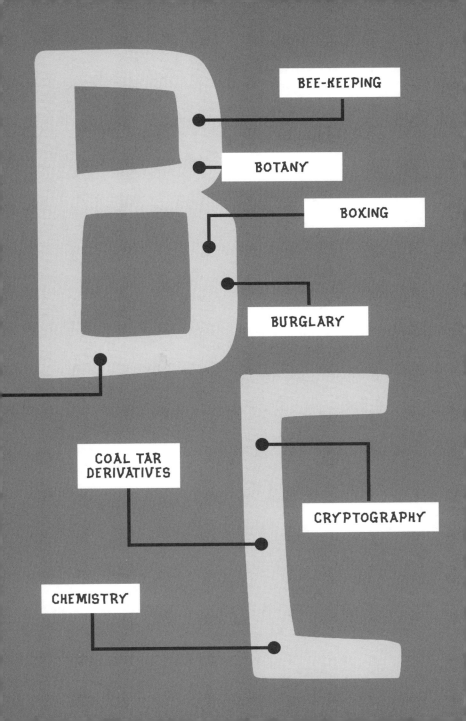

# THE HUMOUR OF HOLMES AND WATSON

Despite the Holmes stories being viewed primarily as 'mysteries', there has always been a good sprinkling of humour in the chronicles of the Great Detective.

*The good Watson had at that time deserted me for a wife, the only selfish action which I can recall in our association.*

'THE BLANCHED SOLDIER'

*'It's quite exciting,' said Sherlock Holmes, with a yawn.*

A STUDY IN SCARLET

VON BORK *He seems to have declared war on the King's English as well as on the English king.*

'HIS LAST BOW'

*I have always held, too, that pistol practice should be distinctly an open-air pastime; and when Holmes, in one of his queer humours, would sit in an armchair with his hair-trigger and a hundred Boxer cartridges and proceed to adorn the opposite wall with a patriotic V.R. done in bullet pocks, I felt strongly that neither the atmosphere nor the appearance of our room was improved by it.*

'THE MUSGRAVE RITUAL'

**LORD ST SIMON**
*I am afraid that it will take wiser heads than yours or mine.*

HOLMES *It is very good of Lord St Simon to honour my head by putting it on a level with his own.*

'THE NOBLE BACHELOR'

LESTRADE *It seemed to me that if the clothes were there the body would not be far off.*

HOLMES *By the same brilliant reasoning, every man's body is to be found in the vicinity of his wardrobe.*

'THE NOBLE BACHELOR'

VON BORK *If I were to shout for help as we passed through the village—*

HOLMES *My dear sir, if you did anything so foolish you would probably enlarge the two limited titles of our village inns by giving us 'The Dangling Prussian' as a signpost.*

'HIS LAST BOW'

# DRAWING SHERLOCK HOLMES

Throughout the long publishing history of Sherlock's adventures, a wide variety of illustrators attempted to add atmosphere and colour to the already excellent stories.

## D.H. FRISTON (1820–1906)

The very first person to draw the Great Detective, for *A Study in Scarlet*, published in *Mrs Beeton's Christmas Annual* in 1887.

## SIDNEY PAGET (1860–1908)

The most famous Sherlock illustrator, Sidney was offered the job by a happy accident – *Strand* intended to ask his younger brother Walter to do the drawings. The magazine never regretted its mistake. It was Paget who introduced what has become the detective's trademark deerstalker hat and cape (never mentioned by Doyle) in his illustrations for 'The Boscombe Valley Mystery'.

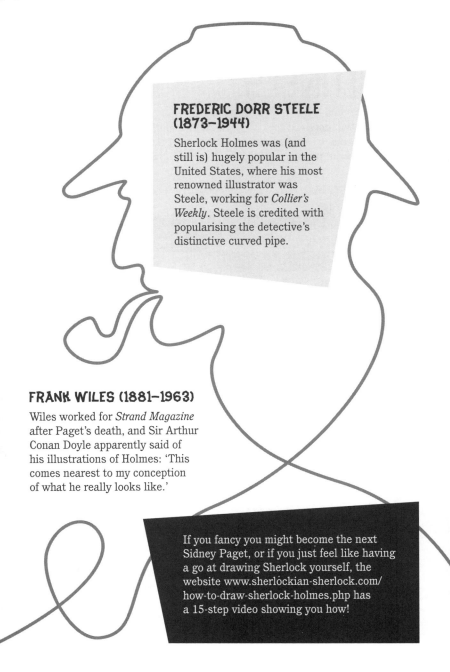

### FREDERIC DORR STEELE (1873–1944)

Sherlock Holmes was (and still is) hugely popular in the United States, where his most renowned illustrator was Steele, working for *Collier's Weekly*. Steele is credited with popularising the detective's distinctive curved pipe.

### FRANK WILES (1881–1963)

Wiles worked for *Strand Magazine* after Paget's death, and Sir Arthur Conan Doyle apparently said of his illustrations of Holmes: 'This comes nearest to my conception of what he really looks like.'

If you fancy you might become the next Sidney Paget, or if you just feel like having a go at drawing Sherlock yourself, the website www.sherlockian-sherlock.com/how-to-draw-sherlock-holmes.php has a 15-step video showing you how!

# COLONELS

With Dr Watson's military background, we should not be surprised
at the number of soldiers who find their way into the stories.
He does seem to have a thing about colonels, though.

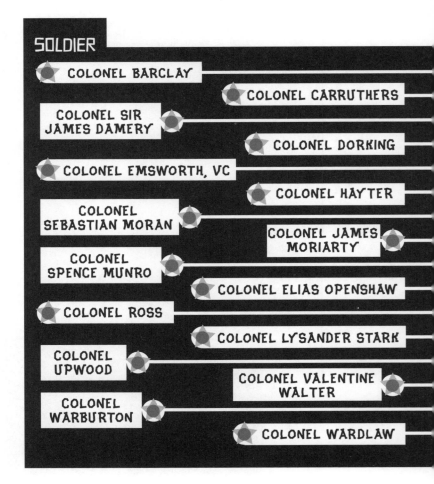

## SOLDIER

COLONEL BARCLAY

COLONEL CARRUTHERS

COLONEL SIR JAMES DAMERY

COLONEL DORKING

COLONEL EMSWORTH, VC

COLONEL HAYTER

COLONEL SEBASTIAN MORAN

COLONEL JAMES MORIARTY

COLONEL SPENCE MUNRO

COLONEL ELIAS OPENSHAW

COLONEL ROSS

COLONEL LYSANDER STARK

COLONEL UPWOOD

COLONEL VALENTINE WALTER

COLONEL WARBURTON

COLONEL WARDLAW

| ROLE | STORY |
|---|---|
| Corpse | 'The Crooked Man' |
| Criminal | 'Wisteria Lodge' |
| Go-between | 'The Illustrious Client' |
| Blackmail victim | 'Charles Augustus Milverton' |
| Concerned father | 'The Blanched Soldier' |
| Old friend of Watson's | 'The Reigate Squires' |
| Moriarty's chief of staff | 'The Empty House' and others |
| Brother of criminal mastermind | 'The Final Problem' |
| Employer | 'The Copper Beeches' |
| Murder victim | 'The Five Orange Pips' |
| Owner of Silver Blaze | 'Silver Blaze' |
| Counterfeiter, murderer | 'The Engineer's Thumb' |
| Card cheat | *The Hound of the Baskervilles* |
| Traitor | 'The Bruce-Partington Plans' |
| Goes mad | Unchronicled |
| Owner of Pugilist | 'Silver Blaze' |

# HIS LAST BOW

The fourth collection of Holmes stories, published in 1917.
'The Adventure of the Cardboard Box', which was described
earlier in *The Memoirs of Sherlock Holmes*, was included
in this collection, having been left out of some editions of
*Memoirs* because of its scandalous content.

## 'Wisteria Lodge'

**FIRST PUBLISHED** *Strand Magazine*, September and October 1908

**MAJOR PLAYERS** Holmes, Watson, John Scott Eccles,
Inspector Baynes, Aloysius Garcia, Don Juan Murillo

**MYSTERY** Published in two distinct parts – 'The Singular
Experience of Mr John Scott Eccles' and 'The Tigers of San
Pedro' – this case, which Holmes himself described as
'chaotic', involves the peculiar night suffered by Scott Eccles in
Wisteria Lodge and the subsequent murder of his young host,
Aloysius Garcia. Inspector Baynes is notable as being the most
impressive police officer Sherlock meets in any of the stories.

## 'The Adventure of the Bruce-Partington Plans'

**FIRST PUBLISHED** *Strand Magazine*, December 1908

**MAJOR PLAYERS** Holmes, Watson, Mycroft Holmes, Arthur Cadogan West, Sir James Walter, Colonel Valentine Walter, Sidney Johnson, Miss Westbury, Hugo Oberstein

**MYSTERY** Those careless civil servants lose yet another set of secret papers, and this time Mycroft enlists Sherlock's help. Seven of the ten missing plans turn up in the pockets of murdered Arthur Cadogan West, a junior clerk at the arsenal where they went missing. The case allows Holmes to perform some truly brilliant deductions, particularly in locating the actual site of the murder.

## 'The Adventure of the Devil's Foot'

**FIRST PUBLISHED** *Strand Magazine*, December 1910

**MAJOR PLAYERS** Holmes, Watson, Leon Sterndale, Mortimer Tregennis, Vicar Roundhay

**MYSTERY** Holmes is on an enforced holiday for his health when he and Watson become involved in the macabre events surrounding the Tregennis family. In his effort to prove the method of the murderer, Sherlock almost kills himself and Watson.

## 'The Adventure of the Red Circle'

**FIRST PUBLISHED** *Strand Magazine*, March and April 1911

**MAJOR PLAYERS** Holmes, Watson, Mrs Warren, Emilia Lucca, Gennaro Lucca, Inspector Gregson, Leverton, Giuseppe Gorgiano

**MYSTERY** A case that begins with the visit of Mrs Warren, a landlady who persuades Holmes to look into the mysterious behaviour of her lodger, a foreign gentleman who never leaves his room. The later abduction and quick release of her husband in a case of mistaken identity adds to the puzzle.

## 'The Disappearance of Lady Frances Carfax'

**FIRST PUBLISHED** *Strand Magazine*, December 1911

**MAJOR PLAYERS** Holmes, Watson, Lady Frances Carfax, Philip Green, Dr Shlessinger, Mrs Shlessinger

**MYSTERY** A case that nearly ends in disaster for Holmes and death for Lady Carfax. As in *The Hound of the Baskervilles*, Sherlock sends Watson to investigate while secretly shadowing him. Holmes is definitely challenged by the problem, realising the solution barely in time.

## 'The Adventure of the Dying Detective'

**FIRST PUBLISHED** *Strand Magazine*, December 1913

**MAJOR PLAYERS** Holmes, Watson, Culverton Smith,
Victor Savage, Inspector Morton

**MYSTERY** Mrs Hudson informs Watson that Sherlock is
dying, having apparently acquired some horrible disease from
the East while 'working among Chinese sailors' in the docks.
Watson wants to consult a medical specialist, but Holmes will
only allow him to bring one man, Culverton Smith, not a doctor
but supposedly an expert on tropical afflictions. The cure is
then rapid.

## 'His Last Bow'

**FIRST PUBLISHED** *Strand Magazine*, September 1917

**MAJOR PLAYERS** Holmes, Watson, Martha, Von Bork,
Von Herling

**MYSTERY** Written in the third person, this is said to be the
result of a question asked by a British general as to what
Holmes might have done during the war. Assuming the
ingenious disguise of the Irish-American agent Altamont,
Sherlock penetrates a dangerous German spy ring headed by
Von Bork.

# THE ONES THAT GOT AWAY

Sherlock comments in April 1891 (in 'The Final Problem') that he has been engaged on over a thousand cases. Considering his remarkable success following his return from Reichenbach, his career casebook

## UNCHRONICLED CASE

The Affair of the Aluminium Crutch

The Bogus Laundry Affair

The Case of the Coptic Patriarchs

The Giant Rat of Sumatra

The Grosvenor Square Furniture Van

The Politician, the Lighthouse and the Trained Cormorant

The Slipshod Elderly Man

The Sudden Death of Cardinal Tosca

Wilson the Canary Trainer

Vanderbilt and the Yeggman

must be at least double this figure. Only 60 cases are chronicled in the series, but Watson tantalises the reader with references to almost a hundred others. Here are the 10 that sound the most intriguing.

## MENTIONED IN

'The Musgrave Ritual'

'The Cardboard Box'

'The Retired Colourman'

'The Sussex Vampire'

'The Noble Bachelor'

'The Veiled Lodger'

'The Five Orange Pips'

'Black Peter'

'Black Peter'

'The Sussex Vampire'

# MORIARTY

Like Mycroft Holmes, the influence of 'the Napoleon of crime' on Sherlock Holmes and his legacy is far out of proportion to his appearance in the stories: Watson sees him only twice, both in 'The Final Problem', first on the platform at Victoria station when Moriarty just fails to board their train, and then from a distance near the Reichenbach Falls. Holmes acknowledged him as being 'a genius' who was almost his intellectual equal (equally telling for illustrating Sherlock's dispassionate assessment of his own ability).

James Moriarty, we learn, is a man of 'good birth and excellent education', a professor of mathematics no less, but Holmes is in no doubt of the reason for his descent into a life of crime, blaming it on 'hereditary tendencies of the most diabolical kind'. The Great Detective's admiration for Moriarty's skills is reciprocated – when Moriarty visits Sherlock to threaten him in 'The Final Problem', he admits 'it would be a grief to me to be forced to take any extreme measure'. Nevertheless, when Holmes successfully dismantles his criminal web, Moriarty seeks to take his revenge on Holmes.

## WHAT MADE HIM SO BAD?

Much speculation has been devoted in books and film to the possible genesis of the Holmes–Moriarty struggle.

| THEORY | SOURCE |
| --- | --- |
| Moriarty was a young Sherlock's maths tutor | *Sherlock Holmes of Baker Street* (W.S. Baring-Gould) |
| Moriarty had an affair with Sherlock's mother | *The Seven-Per-Cent Solution* (Nicholas Meyer) |
| Sherlock caused Moriarty's father to commit suicide | *Enter the Lion* (Sean Wright and Michael Hodel) |
| Moriarty caused the death of young Sherlock's one great love | *Young Sherlock Holmes* (1985 film) |

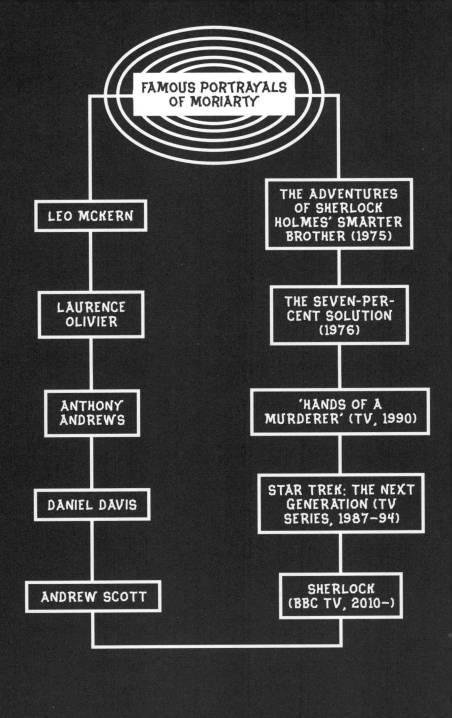

FAMOUS PORTRAYALS OF MORIARTY

LEO MCKERN

LAURENCE OLIVIER

ANTHONY ANDREWS

DANIEL DAVIS

ANDREW SCOTT

THE ADVENTURES OF SHERLOCK HOLMES' SMARTER BROTHER (1975)

THE SEVEN-PER-CENT SOLUTION (1976)

'HANDS OF A MURDERER' (TV, 1990)

STAR TREK: THE NEXT GENERATION (TV SERIES, 1987–94)

SHERLOCK (BBC TV, 2010–)

# SHERLOCK HOLMES AND THE MYSTERY OF THE MISSING DEFINITE ARTICLE

So, is it *The Sign of Four*, or *The Sign of the Four*? The definite article has been in and out of the title almost since the second Sherlock Holmes story first appeared in *Lippincott's Monthly Magazine* in February 1890, when it was certainly 'in'. The story was then republished in several journals as *The Sign of Four*, and the second 'the' was also omitted when Spencer Blackett published the novel in book form in October 1890.

The story itself is little help. Most references (including all the times it is written down by someone) throughout the tale are to 'the sign of the four', but when Small is giving his account he twice refers to 'the sign of four', as does Watson when he reflects on this investigation in 'A Case of Identity' and 'The Five Orange Pips'. Holmes refers to it as 'the Sign of Four' in 'The Stockbroker's Clerk' and 'The Cardboard Box', and Doyle himself uses the shorter version in the preface to *The Case Book of Sherlock Holmes* in 1927.

It appears, then, that Doyle preferred 'The Sign of Four', and that has been the dominant version used in the many presentations and adaptations over the years (for example the BBC's episode of *Sherlock* in 2014 titled 'The Sign of Three'). Some might argue that the most common word in the English language has no need of any extra representation…

# THE VALLEY OF FEAR

## FIRST PUBLISHED

*Strand Magazine*,
September 1914–May
1915; published as a
novel 1915

## MAJOR PLAYERS

Holmes, Watson,
Inspector MacDonald,
John Douglas, Ivy
Douglas, Cecil Barker,
John McMurdo, Ettie
Shafter, Jacob Shafter,
Jack McGinty, Ted Baldwin

# MYSTERY

Presented in two distinct parts, Part One,
'The Tragedy of Birlstone', relates a brilliant
investigation by Holmes into the apparent murder of John
Douglas of Birlstone Manor. Part Two, 'The Scowrers', is
recounted in the third person, presumably by Pinkerton agent
Birdy Edwards, and tells of the evil predators of Vermissa
Valley in the USA and their destruction and arrest.

Its structure is very similar to *A Study in Scarlet*, divided
between Holmes' detection and then a retrospective, brought
together by an epilogue, in this case an unhappy one,
touched by the deadly hand of an old enemy of Sherlock.

*The Valley of Fear* is one of Doyle's least-known
chronicles, certainly overshadowed by the
other three novel-length stories.

# SHERLOCK HOLMES ON THE STAGE

| DATE | PLAY |
|------|------|
| 1893 | *Under the Clock* |
| 1899 | *Sherlock Holmes* |
| 1921 | *The Crown Diamond* |
| 1965 | *Baker Street* |
| 1976 | *Sherlock Holmes* |
| 1977 | *The Marvellous Musical Adventures of Sherlock Holmes* |
| 1978 | *Crucifer of Blood* |
| 1985 | *The Mask of Moriarty* |

Since the first known play to feature Sherlock Holmes in 1893, there have been many theatrical treatments of the Great Detective, some more successful (and respectful) than others.

| AUTHOR | REMARKS |
|---|---|
| Brookfield and Hicks | Earliest known play |
| William Gillette | Best known and most successful |
| Arthur Conan Doyle | Holmes story 'The Mazarin Stone' based on this unsuccessful play |
| James Coopersmith | Musical |
| Gillette revival | Starred *Star Trek*'s Leonard Nimoy |
| William Shrewsbury | Musical |
| Paul Giovanni | Very successful play based on *The Sign of Four* |
| Hugh Leonard | Comedy starring former Doctor Who Tom Baker |

# HI-TECH HOLMES

Sherlock was always one to move with the times and make use of the latest Victorian technology to help him crack a case.

## MAGNIFYING GLASS

Holmes would have been lost without his most precious instrument and his attention to detail with it is legendary, but without the developments in lens technology in the 19th century he would surely not have been able to make some of his devastating observations, such as the 16 characteristics of typewriter characters that he refers to in 'A Case of Identity'.

## GRAMOPHONES

In 'The Mazarin Stone' Holmes fools Count Sylvius and Sam Merton by pretending to play his violin in his bedroom while in fact putting on a record and sneaking back in. He admits, 'These modern gramophones are a remarkable invention.'

## TELEPHONES

Sherlock's career as a consulting detective coincided with the first telephone exchanges being established in London, though if the budding sleuth needed Watson to share his rent in those early days it seems unlikely he could have afforded one of the new-fangled devices. The first mention in the stories is of Inspector Athelney Jones offering to telephone for a police launch in *The Sign of Four*, and Inspector Bradstreet has a telephone in his office in 'The Man with the Twisted Lip', suggesting that the police were early adopters of the technology. The earliest we can be fairly confident that Holmes had his own personal telephone is June 1902 in the case of 'The Three Garridebs', when Watson consults the directory.

## CARS

It appears that Sherlock's only encounter with the internal combustion engine in his adventures comes in his final (chronologically speaking) case, 'His Last Bow', when Watson poses as his chauffeur to drive him to his appointment with Von Bork in 1914. Even then, the German agent mentions that 'he poses as a motor expert', so it seems likely that Holmes has kept up to date with developments.

## TELEGRAMS

The first commercial telegraphy service was laid along 13 miles of the Great Western Railway from Paddington to West Drayton in 1838, and soon grew rapidly along with the expansion of the railways. Sherlock was always ready to use the Victorian version of the email – fast, reliable and to the point.

## RAILWAYS

By the time Sherlock was born in the early
1850s, Great Britain had over 7,000 miles of
railways, an astonishing rate of growth given
that commercial passenger railways had only
been going for 20 years. Armed with his trusty
copy of *Bradshaw*, containing all the train
times he would need, he could confidently
travel all over the country – and at times the
continent – in safety, speed and comfort.

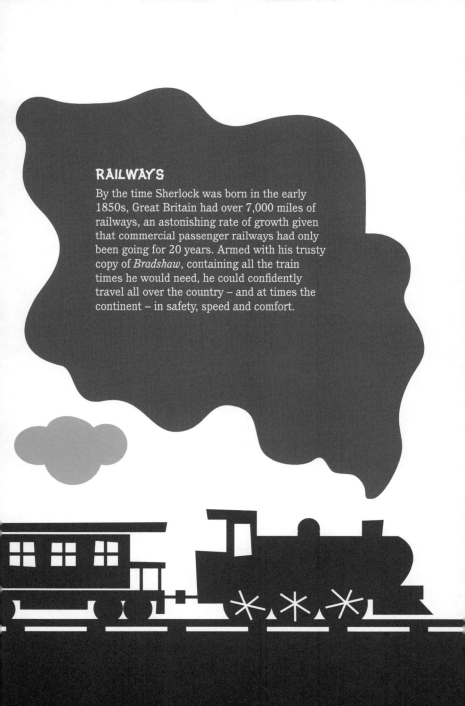

# THE DIOGENES CLUB

A London club situated in Pall Mall of which Mycroft Holmes was a founder member. In 'The Greek Interpreter' Watson is introduced to the club and its very special rules. Realising there was a gap in the market for a club aimed at 'the most unsociable and unclubbable men in town' who are nevertheless 'not averse to comfortable chairs and the latest periodicals', no member is permitted to take any notice of another. Apart from the Stranger's Room, conversation – indeed any talking – is banned, any three offences rendering the culprit liable to expulsion. Sherlock, not surprisingly, found its 'soothing atmosphere' quite appealing.

The club is mentioned on only one other occasion, in 'The Bruce-Partington Plans'. The Diogenes Club has long been a source for speculation and study by Sherlockians and has been considered a possible cover for espionage or secret activities by the British government.

## WHY DIOGENES?

Although it isn't specified in the stories, the club is presumably named after Diogenes the Cynic, a misanthropic Greek philosopher who took to wandering around in daylight with a lamp, claiming to be 'looking for an honest man'. But then, in Doyle's day, one assumes he would have expected his readers to have known that…

# JOSEPH BELL

This gifted medical practitioner, who served as personal surgeon to Queen Victoria whenever she visited Scotland, was one of the leading models for Sherlock Holmes. Arthur Conan Doyle had known him at Edinburgh University, where Bell had been a lecturer and surgeon who also possessed an amazingly acute power of deductive reasoning. Doyle wrote that Bell would sit in the waiting room, diagnosing his visitors as they came in: 'You are a soldier, and a non-commissioned officer at that. You have served in Bermuda.' Bell's activities were so amazing to his students that Conan Doyle looked no further for possible models for a great detective.

In 1882 Doyle dedicated the first collection of Holmes cases, *The Adventures of Sherlock Holmes*, to 'My old teacher, Joseph Bell MD'. Bell, in turn, reviewed the collection for the magazine *Bookman*. In 2000 the BBC broadcast *Murder Rooms: The Dark Beginnings of Sherlock Holmes*, a series of dramas that has a young Conan Doyle assisting Bell (played by Ian Richardson) in solving mysteries.

# CRYPTOGRAPHY

The study of codes or secret writings, of which Holmes was a genuine expert. His knowledge was both demonstrated and tested in 'The Dancing Men', where a substitution cipher was used where stick men represented letters of the alphabet. The code, when broken by Holmes, was used to lure the murderer of Hilton Cubitt to his capture.

There were several other cryptographic puzzles solves by Holmes. In 'The *Gloria Scott*' the coded warning message is:

> *The supply of game for London is going steadily up. Head keeper Hudson, we believe, has been now told to receive all orders for fly-paper and for preservation of your hen pheasant's life.*

See if you can solve it. There's a clue at the bottom of the page*, and if you still can't crack it, the answer is in the 'Whodunnit?' section at the end of the book.

* CLUE: think of the number three.

A little more challenging was the code sent from Porlock, Holmes' agent in the lair of Moriarty in *The Valley of Fear*, which read:

534 C2 13 127 36 31 4 17 21 41
DOUGLAS 109 293 5 37 BIRLSTONE
26 BIRLSTONE 9 47 171

Solving this message depended upon finding the correct book from which the code source was used, with Holmes eventually deducing it would be *Whitaker's Almanack* (so if you've got a copy of *Whitaker's Almanack* from the 1880s lying around – and who hasn't? – have a go at solving it).

# THE CASE BOOK OF SHERLOCK HOLMES

The fifth and final published collection of cases, released in 1927, three years before the death of Sir Arthur Conan Doyle, who remarked in his introduction, 'And so, reader, farewell to Sherlock Holmes!' And this time it really was.

## 'The Adventure of the Mazarin Stone'

**FIRST PUBLISHED** *Strand Magazine*, October 1921

**MAJOR PLAYERS** Holmes, Watson, Billy, Count Negretto Sylvius, Sam Merton

**MYSTERY** One of the least effective and most poorly constructed cases in the series. The Mazarin stone is a great yellow diamond stolen from Whitehall, a crime that brings the prime minister and home secretary, no less, to Baker Street. Because the story is based on a stage play by Doyle, the action is told in the third person and confined to a single room.

## 'The Problem of Thor Bridge'

**FIRST PUBLISHED** *Strand Magazine*, February and March 1922

**MAJOR PLAYERS** Holmes, Watson, J. Neil Gibson, Grace Dunbar, Marlow Bates, Maria Pinto Gibson

**MYSTERY** Holmes is consulted by the American senator and 'Gold King' J. Neil Gibson. His children's governess, Grace Dunbar, has been arrested for the murder of Gibson's wife Maria; despite the damning evidence against her he is convinced of her innocence. Dunbar is eventually cleared by Holmes in one of his cleverest solutions.

## 'The Adventure of the Creeping Man'

**FIRST PUBLISHED** *Strand Magazine*, March 1923

**MAJOR PLAYERS** Holmes, Watson, Professor Presbury, Trevor Bennett, Alice Morphy, Edith Presbury, Dorak, Mercer, Roy

**MYSTERY** One of the most bizarre and badly written entries in the series sees Holmes and Watson engaged in the university town of Camford, where a Professor Presbury has been acting very strangely, culminating in his secretary finding him crawling around on his hands and knees.

## 'The Adventure of the Sussex Vampire'

**FIRST PUBLISHED** *Strand Magazine*, January 1924

**MAJOR PLAYERS** Holmes, Watson, Bob Ferguson, Mrs Ferguson, Mrs Mason, Dolores, Jack Ferguson

**MYSTERY** 'Big' Bob Ferguson is greatly troubled by the inexplicable behaviour of his wife, for she has apparently been caught drinking the blood of her infant son. Crucial to the solution is the condition of the small family dog, Carlo.

### 'The Adventure of the Three Garridebs'

**FIRST PUBLISHED** *Strand Magazine*, January 1925

**MAJOR PLAYERS** Holmes, Watson, Nathan Garrideb, John Garrideb

**MYSTERY** Holmes is engaged by Nathan Garrideb to aid in the search for a third Garrideb, having been told by one John Garrideb, an American lawyer, that should one more Garrideb be found the vast fortune of Alexander Hamilton Garrideb would be shared between them.

### 'The Adventure of the Illustrious Client'

**FIRST PUBLISHED** *Strand Magazine*, November 1924

**MAJOR PLAYERS** Holmes, Watson, Baron Adalbert Gruner, Violet de Merville, Colonel James Damery, Kitty Winter

**MYSTERY** This case presented a believable, reprehensible and utterly vile villain in the person of Baron Gruner, who almost certainly murdered his late wife and is now planning to wed Violet de Merville. It is generally believed that the 'Illustrious Client' who engages Holmes to break up the union is King Edward.

## 'The Adventure of the Three Gables'

**FIRST PUBLISHED** *Strand Magazine*, October 1926

**MAJOR PLAYERS** Holmes, Watson, Mary Maberley, Isadora Klein, Douglas Maberley, Steve Dixie

**MYSTERY** The affair involves the bizarre experience of a widow, Mrs Maberley, the owner of the Three Gables, a villa in Harrow Weald. She is offered a large sum of money for the property, but only if she leaves *everything* in the house to the new owner. Even the few personal belongings she might take must be examined.

## 'The Adventure of the Blanched Soldier'

**FIRST PUBLISHED** *Strand Magazine*, November 1926

**MAJOR PLAYERS** Holmes, James Dodd, Godfrey Emsworth, Colonel Emsworth

**MYSTERY** One of two chronicles written by Holmes himself – the detective ends up leaving the reader as much in the dark as is his custom with Watson, but it does provide some insight into his methods. James Dodd (the 'Blanched Soldier') engages Sherlock to discover why an old friend and comrade, Godfrey Emsworth, has been locked away by his family.

## 'The Adventure of the Lion's Mane'

**FIRST PUBLISHED** *Strand Magazine*, December 1926

**MAJOR PLAYERS** Holmes, Fitzroy McPherson, Ian Murdoch, Harold Stackhurst, Maud Bellamy

**MYSTERY** Written by Holmes, this provides glimpses into his life in retirement. He solves the bizarre and horrible deaths of Fitzroy McPherson and his dog, and the vicious attack on the chief suspect, Ian Murdoch, not through deduction but thanks to his phenomenal memory.

## 'The Adventure of the Retired Colourman'

**FIRST PUBLISHED** *Strand Magazine*, January 1927

**MAJOR PLAYERS** Holmes, Watson, Josiah Amberley, Barker

**MYSTERY** Josiah Amberley comes to Holmes to complain that his wife has apparently left him with her lover, taking with her Amberley's box of deeds. During the case Sherlock demonstrates his skill as a burglar.

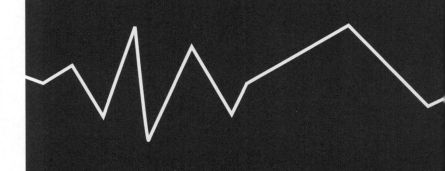

## 'The Adventure of the Veiled Lodger'

**FIRST PUBLISHED** *Strand Magazine*, February 1927

**MAJOR PLAYERS** Holmes, Watson, Eugenia Ronder,
Mrs Merrilow

**MYSTERY** Holmes has little to do in this case, where Mrs
Merrilow brings the puzzle of why her long-term lodger
Eugenia Ronder, who never lifts her veil, has taken to crying
out 'Murder!' She agrees to meet Holmes and he and Watson
travel to Brixton to hear her tragic confession.

## 'The Adventure of Shoscombe Old Place'

**FIRST PUBLISHED** *Strand Magazine*, April 1927

**MAJOR PLAYERS** Holmes, Watson, Sir Robert Norberton,
John Mason

**MYSTERY** Head trainer at Shoscombe John Mason comes to
Holmes complaining about his employer, Sir Robert Norberton,
who appears to have gone mad under the pressure to produce
a Derby winner. A further puzzle is that Lady Beatrice Falder,
Sir Robert's sister, has not been seen in person for some time,
and Sir Robert has given away her pet spaniel. The beloved dog
helps solve all.

# HOLMES ON THE WEB

As you might imagine, there is now a plethora of websites dedicated to the Great Detective, some commercial enterprises, some very much fan-based. Here are just a few.

**www.thescienceofdeduction.co.uk**
Tie-in to the BBC's *Sherlock* series

**www.sherlock-holmes.co.uk**
Website of the Sherlock Holmes Museum

**www.sherlockian.net**
Comprehensive fan website

**www.sherlockology.com**
Unofficial fan site of BBC's *Sherlock*

**www.sherlock-holmes.org.uk**
The Sherlock Holmes Society of London

**www.johnwatsonblog.co.uk**
The contemporary equivalent of Watson's notebooks (BBC's *Sherlock*)

**www.sherlockholmesonline.org**
The official website of the Sir Arthur Conan Doyle literary estate

**www.diogenes-club.com**
Enthusiast website

**www.fanfiction.net/book/Sherlock-Holmes**
Want new Sherlock stories? Look no further

**www.siracd.com**
Devoted to the life and work of Sir
Arthur Conan Doyle

**www.redcircledc.org**
'Sherlock's home in Washington DC'

**www.ash-nyc.com**
The Adventuresses of Sherlock Holmes, 'the
oldest women's Sherlockian society'

**bakerstreetbabes.com**
For a more modern female take on Holmes

**www.bakerstreetjournal.com**
'The premier publication of scholarship about
Sherlock Holmes'

**always1895.net**
For more Sherlock Holmes links

# THREE CLASSIC SHERLOCKS

### BASIL RATHBONE (1892–1967)

This English actor became the most beloved and recognised portrayor of Sherlock Holmes through his numerous film and stage appearances and his long-running radio programme. While this earned him a huge following, it was also a terrible burden and a deep frustration for the Shakespearean-trained actor. His first outing as Sherlock was in the 1939 *Hound of the Baskervilles*, and 13 more films were to follow. By 1946, Rathbone had tired of Holmes and despaired of ever freeing himself from the role. Although he would occasionally return to the character in later years, he chose not to renew his film and radio contracts, much to the disappointment of his Watson, actor Nigel Bruce.

## JEREMY BRETT (1933–95)

Appearing as the Great Detective on television between 1984 and 1994, in Granada Television's faithful and authentic adaptation of the original stories, Brett's performance as Holmes is considered by many to be the finest of all time, surpassing even Rathbone's. The actor once said, 'Sherlock Holmes is a free spirit, you cannot pin him down – he is probably the most complicated character I've played in my life.' As with Rathbone, the character seemed to overwhelm Brett; the difference was that he embraced it rather than shying away.

## BENEDICT CUMBERBATCH (1976–)

This very 21st-century Holmes is *the* Sherlock for the younger generation of Holmes fans, starring in the acclaimed and award-laden *Sherlock* for BBC television since 2010, a modern re-imagining of the character by writers Steven Moffat and Mark Gatiss. Despite his close association with the Great Detective in the eyes of Holmes enthusiasts, Cumberbatch's impressive body of film and television work both before and since winning the role means he is unlikely to suffer the typecasting fate of Rathbone and Brett.

# THE MAXIMS OF SHERLOCK HOLMES

In his capacity as Boswell to Sherlock's Johnson, Dr Watson recorded a number of sayings of the Great Detective that are now famous. The most famous of all, 'Elementary, my dear Watson,' was not actually uttered by Holmes in any of the stories.

*Genius is an infinite capacity for taking pains.*

A STUDY IN SCARLET

*To a great mind, nothing is little.*

A STUDY IN SCARLET

*When you have eliminated the impossible, whatever remains, however improbable, must be the truth.*

THE SIGN OF FOUR

*As a rule, the more bizarre a thing is the less mysterious is proves to be.*

'THE RED-HEADED LEAGUE'

*It is my business to know things.*

'A CASE OF IDENTITY'

*It is, of course, a trifle, but there is nothing so important as trifles.*

'THE MAN WITH THE TWISTED LIP'

*I am not retained by the police to supply their deficiencies.*

'THE BLUE CARBUNCLE'

**Come, Watson, come!
The Game is afoot!**

'THE ABBEY GRANGE'

HOLMES *I followed you.*

STERNDALE *I saw no one.*

HOLMES *That is what you may expect to see when I follow you.*

'THE DEVIL'S FOOT'

# SIR ARTHUR CONAN DOYLE (1859–1930)

A Scottish physician, writer and novelist, the creator of Sherlock Holmes was also an avid sportsman, a war correspondent and an ardent student of spiritualism.

One of ten children, Arthur's alcoholic father meant his was a far from ideal upbringing. After spending a year in Austria he studied medicine at Edinburgh University under Dr Joseph Bell, his inspiration for the character of the Great Detective. After holding several jobs, he joined a former schoolmate in practice in Plymouth, but soon set up independently as an oculist. His lack of patients gave him plenty of free time to indulge his passion for writing.

He didn't settle on the character of Holmes until 1887, when *A Study in Scarlet* was published, which brought him the sum of £25 (no royalties). A follow-up was commissioned, leading to *The Sign of Four*, and in 1891 he set about writing more Holmes stories for *Strand Magazine*. The reaction was more than Doyle could have hoped for, but within two years he had grown so tired of Holmes that he decided the time had come to kill him off, complaining that it 'takes my mind from better things'.

In 1900 Doyle sailed for Cape Town to serve as a medical officer in the Boer War. He believed it was his support for the war that won him a knighthood in 1902. His first wife died in 1906 and Doyle remarried the following year. One of the honoured guests at his wedding was George Edalji, whom Doyle had helped free from prison and wrongful prosecution, one of the many real-life investigations that people routinely brought to him as the creator of the Great Detective.

After writing *The Hound of the Baskervilles* in 1901, a new Holmes story set before the events of 'The Final Problem', Doyle bowed to pressure and brought Sherlock back to life in 1903. He would continue to write new Holmes stories for the next 24 years. What obsessed him for the final years of his life, particularly from 1916, was spiritualism, and he authored some 30 books on the subject. He died on 7 July 1930 after a severe heart attack. Although he had promised to send a message from beyond the grave to his loved ones, no such communication has, apparently, ever arrived.

## FIVE DOYLE NOVELS YOU'VE PROBABLY NEVER HEARD OF

*Micah Clarke* (1888)
*The White Company* (1891)
*Rodney Stone* (1896)
*Uncle Bernac* (1897)
*Sir Nigel* (1906)

## ONE DOYLE NOVEL YOU JUST MIGHT HAVE HEARD OF

*The Lost World* (1912)

# DOYLE'S DISTINGUISHED DOZEN

In 1927, *Strand Magazine* attempted to answer the question: 'Which Sherlock Holmes stories are the best?' At the request of the magazine, Conan Doyle chose 12 stories from the 44 that had by then been published in book form (not including the novels) that he considered superior. A contest was held for readers to identify which ones they thought he would select. The winner matched 10 of the 12, and Conan Doyle's own list (below) was published in the June edition.

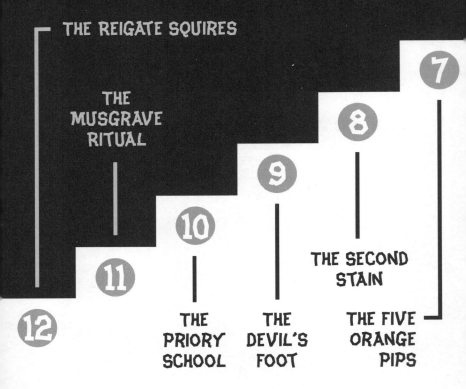

THE REIGATE SQUIRES

THE MUSGRAVE RITUAL

7

8

9

10

11

12

THE SECOND STAIN

THE PRIORY SCHOOL

THE DEVIL'S FOOT

THE FIVE ORANGE PIPS

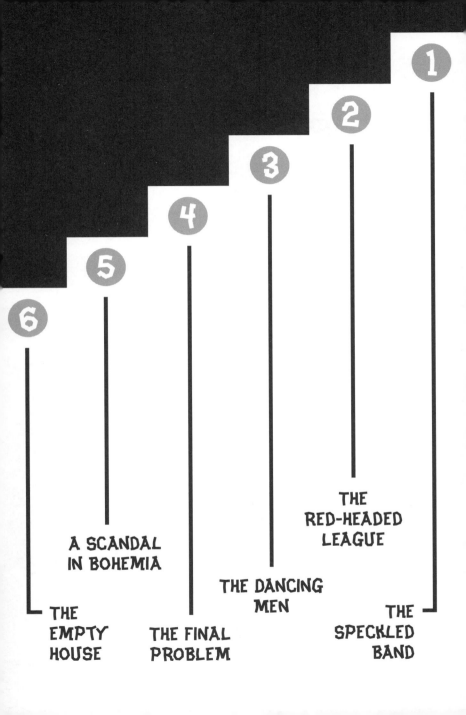

1
THE
SPECKLED
BAND

2
THE
RED-HEADED
LEAGUE

3
THE DANCING
MEN

4
THE FINAL
PROBLEM

5
A SCANDAL
IN BOHEMIA

6
THE
EMPTY
HOUSE

# A SHERLOCKIAN LIBRARY

Since Conan Doyle's death in 1930, literary interest in the Great Detective has never stopped. Here are books from every decade since Doyle's demise that have sought to exploit or shed light on some aspect of Sherlock Holmes:

## 1930s

**SHERLOCK HOLMES: FACT OR FICTION?**

T. S. BLAKENEY
(John Murray, 1932)

## 1940s

**A BAKER STREET FOUR-WHEELER: SIXTEEN PIECES OF SHERLOCKIANA**

EDGAR W. SMITH (ED.)
(The Pamphlet House, 1944)

## 1950s

**A DOCTOR ENJOYS SHERLOCK HOLMES**

EDWARD J. VAN LIERE
(Vantage Press, 1959)

**1960s**

SHERLOCK HOLMES: A CENTENARY CELEBRATION

ALLEN EYLES
(John Murray, 1966)

**1970s**

SHERLOCK HOLMES: TEN LITERARY STUDIES

TREVOR H. HALL
(St Martin's Press, 1970)

**1980s**

SHERLOCK HOLMES IN AMERICA

BILL BLACKBEARD
(Harry N. Abrams, 1981)

**1990s**

THE LIFE AND TIMES OF SHERLOCK HOLMES

PHILIP WELLER AND
CHRISTOPHER RODEN
(Crescent, 1993)

**2000s**

THE SHERLOCK HOLMES WALK

PAUL KENNETH GARNER
(Louis London Walks, 2000)

**2010s**

A BEDSIDE BOOK OF EARLY SHERLOCKIAN
PARODIES AND PASTICHES

CHARLES PRESS
(MX Publishing, 2014)

# CHRONOLOGY OF HOLMES AND WATSON

In the mid-20th century, William Stuart Baring-Gould plotted the likely dates of significant events in the lives of the main players in the Sherlock Holmes stories, using a combination of analysis of Doyle's writings and a little educated guesswork.

**7 AUG 1852**
John Watson born

**6 JAN 1854**
Sherlock Holmes born

**SEP 1872**
Watson enters University of London Medical School

**OCT 1872**
Holmes enters university (perhaps Christ Church, Oxford)

**AUG-SEP 1874**
Holmes solves his first case ('The *Gloria Scott*')

**1877/8**
Holmes moves to London and begins his career as a consulting detective

**NOV 1878**
Watson attached to the Fifth Northumberland Fusiliers; outbreak of Second Afghan War

**23 NOV 1879**
Possible departure of Holmes to America in the guise of an actor(!)

**27 JUL 1880**
Watson wounded at Battle of Maiwand

**5 AUG 1880**
Holmes returns to England

## JAN 1881
Holmes and Watson meet for the first time

## OCT 1901
Watson marries for a third time

## NOV 1886
Watson marries Constance Adams

## 1903
Holmes retires to the Sussex Downs

## DEC 1887
Death of first Mrs Watson

## 1912/13
Holmes agrees to help the British government track down German spies

## MAY 1889
Watson marries Mary Morstan

## 1914
Watson rejoins the army as a physician

## 4 MAY 1891
Holmes and Moriarty have their fatal tussle at Reichenbach

## 24 JUL 1929
Death of Dr Watson

## 1891/2
Death of second Mrs Watson

## 19 NOV 1946
Death of Mycroft Holmes

## 5 APR 1894
Holmes returns to Baker Street

## 6 JAN 1957
Death of Sherlock Holmes

# WHODUNNIT?

SPOILER ALERT! If you just can't find time to work your way through Sherlock's various cases – although you really should – here's a potted digest of how each story ends. Look away now if you don't want to know!

## THE NOVELS

### A STUDY IN SCARLET

Jefferson Hope's sweetheart was snatched from him many years ago in America by Drebber and Stangerson, who also killed her father. Encountering them in London, he takes his revenge by offering each the choice of two pills, one poisoned, the other inert (while Hope takes the other). His aortic aneurysm kills him before he can appear in court, but he dies content.

### The Sign of Four

The 'Sign of the Four' is an agreement between Jonathan Small, Tonga and two other accomplices, betrayed by Major Sholto, and is found scribbled on a note pinned to Major Sholto's chest after his death and beside the body of his son Bartholomew Sholto after his murder. Sholto Jr had at last found his father's ill-gotten treasure, and was killed by Tonga when he and Small robbed him of it. During the exciting river chase, Tonga is shot and killed by Holmes and Watson; Small is apprehended. The treasure ends up at the bottom of the Thames.

## THE HOUND OF THE BASKERVILLES

A battle for inheritance is at the bottom of this mystery.
Sir Henry is not in fact the last of the Baskervilles – there is
another nephew of Sir Charles who will inherit if he can get rid
of Henry. Taking the name of Stapleton, he had used a ferocious
hound daubed with phosphorus to prey on Sir Charles' fears;
the baronet had a fatal heart attack running from the beast.
Holmes sends Watson to Dartmoor but secretly follows and
sets himself up on the moor to observe events in secret. A side
plot and red herring is the appearance on the moor of another
mysterious character, escaped murderer Selden, who turns
out to be the brother of Mrs Barrymore, the butler's wife at
Baskerville Hall. Selden perishes after being pursued by the
hound, as he is wearing some old clothes of Sir Charles's. A
thrilling climax in Grimpen Mire ends with the hound being
shot as it attacks Sir Henry. Stapleton is assumed to have been
sucked into the unforgiving clutches of the marsh.

## The Valley of Fear

John Douglas, a former Pinkerton agent but now a rich man who
changed his identity and came to England to escape people he
helped to convict, blows the head off a man sent to kill him and
switches clothes in an attempt to pose as dead and throw his
enemies off the scent. Holmes solves the mystery after noting a
missing dumbbell and deducing something must be hidden in the
moat of Douglas's residence. Douglas (aka Birdy Edwards, aka
McMurdo) comes out of hiding to recount his tale of the desperate
goings-on in the Vermissa Valley years earlier, where the vicious
Scowrers were finally brought to justice. Although the worst were
hanged, enough survived to pursue Douglas for vengeance.

In an unhappy postscript, Douglas, having had his plea of self-
defence accepted, flees England on Sherlock's advice but vanishes
from his ship, supposedly washed overboard in a gale. Holmes
believes it was no accident: 'I can tell a Moriarty when I see one.'

# THE SHORT STORIES

## 'A SCANDAL IN BOHEMIA'

Irene Adler retains the incriminating photograph Sherlock is after, but promises not to use it.

## 'The Red-Headed League'

Holmes realises that it is a ploy to remove the pawnbroker from his shop so a gang of thieves can dig a tunnel to the bank next door, and the Red-Headed League is caught red-handed.

## 'A CASE OF IDENTITY'

By comparing two typewritten letters, Sherlock proves that Hosmer Angel was in fact Mary Sutherland's wicked stepfather Windibank in disguise, determined to hold on to her inheritance. He chooses not to illuminate Mary, saying, 'If I tell her she will not believe me.'

## 'The Boscombe Valley Mystery'

John Turner, a former highway robber in Australia, kills his blackmailer Charles McCarthy, a man whose life he once spared after robbing a wagon train. When he learns Turner is ill and has not long to live, Sherlock declines to hand him over to the police.

### 'The Five Orange Pips'

Holmes identifies the murderers of John Openshaw, led by Captain Calhoun, but they have already boarded a ship for America. Sherlock telegrams ahead for them to be arrested on arrival, but the ship sinks in the Atlantic.

### 'THE MAN WITH THE TWISTED LIP'

After all Sherlock's exertions, the missing man, Neville St Clair, is eventually discovered to have been moonlighting as a professional (and highly successful) beggar.

### 'The Adventure of the Blue Carbuncle'

Holmes sets off on a tame goose chase to clear John Horner's name of theft. Having discovered that the culprit is the hotel attendant James Ryder and that it was an opportunistic act, he lets him off – well, it is Christmas.

### 'The Adventure of the Speckled Band'

The evil Grimesby Roylott is planning to kill Helen Stoner in the same manner as he murdered her sister Julia, via a lethal swamp adder, but Holmes successfully turns the tables, and the snake, on him.

### 'THE ADVENTURE OF THE ENGINEER'S THUMB'

Holmes deduces that the murderous mischief is down to a gang of counterfeiters, but he arrives to find their hideout in flames and the criminals gone. A rare occasion on which Sherlock's opponents escape justice.

## 'THE ADVENTURE OF THE NOBLE BACHELOR'

It transpires no crime has been committed; Hatty has in fact run off with her first husband, who she quite reasonably thought had been killed by Apaches until she saw him at her wedding.

### 'The Adventure of the Beryl Coronet'

Alexander Holder's niece Mary has been seduced by Sir George Burnwell – 'one of the most dangerous men in England', according to Holmes – and helps him steal the coronet. Arthur Holder retrieves it, minus three stones, but is too much of a gentleman to clear himself by incriminating his cousin, whom he loves. Holmes solves the case and retrieves the gems, but the despicable Burnwell is not brought to account.

### 'The Adventure of the Copper Beeches'

Jephro Rucastle has locked up his daughter to stop her marrying and taking her money with her, and hires Violet Hunter as a lookalike to throw her fiancé off the scent. He proves as determined as Sherlock though, and all ends well, except for the greedy father who only just survives an attack by his own dog.

### 'SILVER BLAZE'

One of those cases in which the victim is also the villain. Deceased trainer John Straker was in the act of knobbling Silver Blaze out on the moor when the horse kicked out, delivering a fatal blow to his head. The four-legged killer then wandered off and was safely looked after by a neighbour until the big race.

## 'The Adventure of the Cardboard Box'

You almost end up feeling sorry for the pathetic killer, Jim Browner, who murders his wife and her lover, then cuts her ears off and sends them to her scheming sister Sarah, although they end up being opened by the blameless third sister, Susan. No wonder this story was thought too scandalous at the time to stay in the *Memoirs* collection for long.

## 'THE ADVENTURE OF THE YELLOW FACE'

Holmes is convinced that the mystery occupant of the cottage is Effie's first husband, not dead as she insists, but returned from America to blackmail her. Grant Munro breaks down the door with Holmes and Watson in attendance, only to find a child wearing a yellow mask, which reveals a little black girl. It is Effie's child; his wife had feared her husband's reaction. In fact, when he learns the facts, Munro lifts the girl up and kisses her.

## 'THE ADVENTURE OF THE STOCKBROKER'S CLERK'

In a variation on the Red-Headed League, Pycroft is diverted to Birmingham so an imposter can take his place in order to rob the strong room at a stockbroker's. But he is caught by the police on leaving the London premises with the loot, and Sherlock apprehends the accomplice. The two criminals are in fact brothers, but a shortage of gang members led them to invent another one in an attempt to deceive Pycroft.

## 'THE ADVENTURE OF THE GLORIA SCOTT'

'The game is up. Hudson has told all. Fly for your life!' That is the message revealed if you read every third word of the message received by Victor Trevor Sr, telling him that his secret life as a transported convict was about to be revealed, and causing the stroke that proved fatal. The devious blackmailer Hudson was never heard of again.

## 'The Adventure of the Musgrave Ritual'

Holmes reasons correctly, as Brunton the butler did, that the ritual was in fact a riddle. Having solved that, he discovers Brunton's body in a secret treasure chamber beneath a heavy slab. Having unwisely enlisted Rachel Howells (who hated him) to help him lift it, it seems she either deliberately let it fall to entomb him or else made no effort to get help when it happened by accident. She vanished that night and never came back.

## 'THE ADVENTURE OF THE REIGATE SQUIRES'

The spate of burglaries is used as a smokescreen by father and son murderers. The Cunninghams do away with Kirwin to stop him blackmailing them over their dishonest activities.

## 'The Adventure of the Crooked Man'

Barclay died of an apoplectic fit on seeing an old army colleague he had betrayed to the enemy years before – he hit his head in the fall. The small creature was a mongoose, belonging to the 'Crooked Man', Henry Wood.

## 'The Adventure of the Resident Patient'

Blessington is a former bank robber and police informer, whose evidence caused the execution of one of his former gang and the imprisonment of the others. They finally catch up with him, 'try' him, and sentence him to death.

## 'THE ADVENTURE OF THE GREEK INTERPRETER'

Kemp and Latimer, two nasty pieces of work, are trying to get Paul Kratides to sign over some property for them to profit from, but need an interpreter. When they realise Meles has called in the authorities and they are discovered, they abduct him again, leaving the interpreter in a gas-filled room with Kratides (who dies as a result), and flee. They later come to a sticky end in Hungary.

## 'The Adventure of the Naval Treaty'

The villain of the piece is Percy Phelps' prospective brother-in-law Joseph, who has lost money playing the stock market. The reason the treaty has not been sold on is that it was hidden in the room where Phelps' sister kindly put Percy to recuperate!

## 'THE FINAL PROBLEM'

For once, it was Sherlock Holmes that did it! He not only rid the world of the evil Moriarty, but he faked his own death in order to wrong-foot a host of criminals who he would pursue anonymously for the next three years of his career.

## 'The Adventure of the Empty House'

Adair's killer is none other than crack shot Colonel Sebastian Moran, one of Moriarty's henchmen who eluded the round-up of his gang. He faced exposure as a card sharp by Adair and shot him with a powerful air gun.

## 'The Adventure of the Norwood Builder'

Oldacre fakes his own murder in an attempt to gain revenge on McFarlane's mother, who once spurned his advances, by framing her son. He might have got away with it without the fake thumbprint, as Sherlock knew that it had not been present when he inspected the property the previous day. Suspecting a hidden room, he smokes out his man.

## 'THE ADVENTURE OF THE DANCING MEN'

Holmes uses frequency analysis to crack the code, by which time the messages have turned threatening. He hurries to Norfolk but is too late. Elsie's former fiancé Abe Slaney (she left him because of his criminal activities) has turned up from America to claim her. Hilton Cubitt fires at him and he responds, killing the Englishman. Elsie then shoots herself in despair, but recovers.

## 'THE ADVENTURE OF THE SOLITARY CYCLIST'

A complicated plot noteworthy for Sherlock's punch-up in a pub with Jack Woodley. Violet, unknown to her, is a potentially wealthy heiress, and Woodley and his accomplice abduct and force her into a sham (and illegal) marriage. Holmes turns up just in time to apprehend them, but can't prevent Carruthers, the 'Solitary Cyclist' who is actually Violet's protector, from shooting and wounding Woodley.

## 'The Adventure of the Priory School'

A tangled web of family misfortune: the man behind the abduction is the Duke's illegitimate son, Wilder, and the kidnapper he hires killed Heidegger when he followed them. Wilder in dismay confesses to his father and returns the boy, but they keep it secret to allow Hayes, the murderer, time to escape for fear of scandal. Holmes solves the puzzle, realises the Duke's complicity and cheerfully relieves him of a handsome cheque. Hayes is apprehended and faces the gallows.

## 'THE ADVENTURE OF BLACK PETER'

It is obvious to Holmes that the slight figure of Neligan could never have driven a harpoon through a man's body and into the wall of Black Peter's cabin. To find who could have, he poses as Captain Basil and advertises for a harpoon expert, and Patrick Cairns falls into his trap.

## 'The Adventure of Charles Augustus Milverton'

Just as Sherlock is about to retrieve the documents from Milverton's safe, he and Watson secretly witness one of the blackmailer's former victims shoot him dead – Holmes prevents Watson from going to his assistance. He then burns all the safe's contents before they make their escape.

## 'The Adventure of the Six Napoleons'

Beppo the bust-smasher is searching for a stolen gem he hid inside a soft plaster-cast just before his arrest. The murder victim was a former associate on his trail.

## 'THE ADVENTURE OF THE THREE STUDENTS'

No grisly goings-on for a change; by identifying the clay as having come from the athletics jumping pit, and deducing from the scratch on the desk which way the culprit fled, Holmes is able to point the finger of guilt at Gilchrist, the athlete. The noble servant Bannister helped cover up for him but then persuades him to confess, and all ends happily as Gilchrist withdraws from the examination to join the Rhodesian Police.

## 'THE ADVENTURE OF THE GOLDEN PINCE-NEZ'

The secretary was killed accidentally in a struggle by the estranged wife of the professor, who was then hidden by him in his study. Holmes used the cigarette ash to track her footprints when she came out of her hiding place behind the bookcase. On detection, the poor woman takes poison and dies.

## 'THE ADVENTURE OF THE MISSING THREE-QUARTER'

Tragedy without crime in this tale, because when Holmes tracks down Godfrey Staunton by means of spraying aniseed on Dr Armstrong's carriage wheels, he finds him grieving at the bedside of his recently departed wife. Staunton had concealed the marriage because he knew his father would have disapproved.

## 'The Adventure of the Abbey Grange'

Although Holmes is at first content to accept the obvious solution that robbers are to blame, after mulling it over on the train he changes his mind and returns straightaway to Abbey Grange. Working it all out, he confronts sea captain Jack Croker, who admits to killing Brackenstall in self-defence as he attacked his wife. So impressed is Holmes that he appoints himself as judge and Watson as jury. 'Not guilty' is the verdict.

## 'THE ADVENTURE OF THE SECOND STAIN'

Lady Hilda, Trelawney Hope's wife, stole the papers from her husband because she was being blackmailed by the agent Lucas. He was murdered by his wife who thought he was having an affair with Lady Hilda. Holmes retrieves the papers and succeeds in restoring them to the box from which they were stolen, without incriminating the lady.

## 'WISTERIA LODGE'

Scott Eccles wakes in Wisteria Lodge to find it deserted. Holmes reasons that the clocks were tampered with to give Garcia an alibi for something which led to his demise as he sought revenge on Don Juan Murillo, former evil dictator of San Pedro, now on the run from his enemies. Murillo escapes again, but we learn at the end that he has been murdered in Madrid.

## 'The Adventure of the Bruce-Partington Plans'

Cadogan West, far from trying to steal the plans, was killed while trying to retrieve them by the agent Oberstein. Holmes works out that his body, rather than falling from a train compartment, was placed on the roof and fell off as the carriage went over some points. From this he deduces the location of the murder. The traitorous Colonel Valentine, who stole the plans for Oberstein, dies in prison.

## 'The Adventure of the Devil's Foot'

The 'Devil's Foot' is the poisonous root with which Mortimer Tregennis kills his sister and drives mad his brothers, and which is then used by Dr Sterndale to kill Mortimer in revenge. Holmes tests the root's properties and is immediately overcome, only being saved by Watson's quick actions.

## 'The Adventure of the Red Circle'

The mysterious lodger has been replaced by an Italian lady, and she and her husband are on the run from a criminal gang. Her husband kills the assassin who has been sent for them in a fight, and though Inspector Gregson is on hand to question the couple, it seems unlikely they will be charged.

## 'THE DISAPPEARANCE OF LADY FRANCES CARFAX'

Kidnapped for jewels by an Australian conman posing as a missionary, Lady Carfax has been chloroformed and is about to be buried in a coffin until Holmes steps in. The conman, Holy Peters, who was too squeamish to murder her but would have let her die slowly in the coffin, escapes.

## 'The Adventure of the Dying Detective'

Sherlock, of course, is only feigning mortal illness to entrap a confession from Culverton Smith, who killed his own nephew and has recently sent a poisoned box to Holmes to prevent him investigating further. As with his faked death at Reichenbach, the Great Detective omits to take Watson into his confidence, as 'among your many talents dissimulation finds no place'.

## 'HIS LAST BOW'

As this is more a spy story than a mystery, there is no whodunnit here. Holmes has come out of bee-keeping retirement to answer his country's call, arresting several foreign agents and finally revealing to Von Bork the worthlessness of all the information he has been passed (which seems a rather elementary mistake to make if you want your enemy to carry on believing it, but still...)

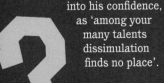

## 'THE ADVENTURE OF THE MAZARIN STONE'

Holmes has already solved the mystery of whodunnit at the beginning of the story – it was Count Sylvius. All that remains is for him to find the whereabouts of the diamond, which he does by repeating the wax dummy trick from 'The Empty Room' combined with a secret door in his rooms (that we have never come across before) and the ingenious use of state-of-the-art technology – a gramophone.

## 'The Problem of Thor Bridge'

Gibson was in an unhappy marriage and had fallen in love with Miss Dunbar. Enraged upon discovering her husband's affections for the governess, Maria Gibson had committed suicide in such a manner as to frame Dunbar, the revolver she used being whisked into the lake by means of a rock on a piece of string after she had fired it.

## 'The Adventure of the Creeping Man'

It transpires that the professor is engaged to a young lady and, in an attempt to rediscover his youthful vigour, has been taking a quack serum derived from langur monkeys. This has had the unfortunate side effect of making him behave like one.

## 'The Adventure of the Sussex Vampire'

Holmes announces that he solved the case before leaving Baker Street – 'the rest has merely been observation and confirmation'. Far from sucking her baby's blood to drink it, Mrs Ferguson has been sucking out poison from a dart fired by the infant's malevolent step-brother.

### 'THE ADVENTURE OF THE THREE GARRIDEBS'

There is only one Garrideb – Nathan. The American is James Winter, a fugitive from justice who has killed several times, including the former occupant of Nathan's rooms; he is trying by elaborate means to get Nathan out of the way while he searches for a stash of counterfeit notes left there. In the course of a struggle he is apprehended, but not before shooting Watson in the leg.

## 'THE ADVENTURE OF THE ILLUSTRIOUS CLIENT'

Even when Violet is introduced to Kitty Winter, a lady the Baron has misused terribly, she refuses to believe ill of her vile fiancée. Holmes decides to steal the Baron's incriminating 'lust diary'; as he does so, Kitty throws acid in the Baron's face. The diary has the intended effect and the wedding is called off.

## 'The Adventure of the Three Gables'

Mrs Maberley's son has written a novel, a thinly disguised account of a liaison he had with the wealthy Isadora Klein. Klein is desperate to suppress it by any means, including burglary and intimidation, and finally succeeds in burning it, although Holmes makes her compensate Mrs Maberley with a round-the-world cruise.

## 'THE ADVENTURE OF THE BLANCHED SOLDIER'

Poor Godfrey Emsworth has contracted what appears to be leprosy and has to be isolated from his terrified and embarrassed family. Holmes brings an eminent dermatologist to examine him and he brings the good news that the condition is pseudo-leprosy – and quite curable.

## 'THE ADVENTURE OF THE LION'S MANE'

An apparently complicated love triangle between McPherson, Murdoch and Maud Bellamy throws everyone off the scent, but Sherlock's knowledge of natural history finally enables him to solve the riddle of McPherson's agonising death. A Lion's Mane jellyfish has been washed into the lagoon used by the victim as a bathing pond.

## 'The Adventure of the Retired Colourman'

A case where Watson's observational powers are acknowledged by Holmes for once. Josiah Amberley has in fact murdered his wife and her lover in the basement, then dumped their bodies in the well. So why does he himself call in Sherlock Holmes? 'Pure swank!' according to the Great Detective.

## 'The Adventure of the Veiled Lodger'

Holmes remembers the case of Ronder, a circus showman supposedly killed by his own lion some years before. Eugenia Ronder confesses that her lover Leonardo murdered her brutal husband, but when she released the lion to make it look as though the animal had done it, the beast turned on her and mauled her terribly. Now she has learned of Leonardo's death, she wants to confess. Holmes does not inform the police – her pain and disfigurement has been punishment enough.

## 'THE ADVENTURE OF SHOSCOMBE OLD PLACE'

Lady Beatrice died of natural causes, but as she is the only person between Sir Robert and his debtors, he covers it up to give him chance to win the Derby and restore his fortune. Sherlock cracks the case by finding the dog and taking it back to the estate to observe its reaction. Sir Robert comes out of the affair perhaps rather better than he deserved, winning the race and getting only a 'mild censure' from the police.

'I HAD NO IDEA THAT SUCH INDIVIDUALS DID EXIST OUTSIDE OF STORIES.'

Dr Watson on
Sherlock Holmes,
A Study in Scarlet